Embrace the Rain

Michael Holloway Perronne

Embrace the Rain

Published by Chances Press, Los Angeles, CA.

www.chancespress.com

This novel is dedicated to my grandmother, Wilhelmena Holloway,

who has always taught her family, that above all else,

what matters most is what's in your heart.

Prologue

There is not much that can compete with the sheer majesty of a hundreds-year-old oak tree. Symbolizing strength and continuing growth, the tree's massiveness inspires awe, especially in children who feel compelled to climb its sturdy branches as generations had done before.

Kate remembered being a little girl heading to the beach and walking across the hot asphalt along Beach Boulevard in Long Beach, Mississippi. Her mother, still youthful, with hair the color of red clay and rosy cheeks, held her hand as they dashed across the first side of the highway to the median.

"We have to wait for the cars," her mother reminded her, when Kate started to make a mad dash across the boulevard. Just the anticipation of building one of their grand sandcastles together had had Kate awake since early morning.

Kate always loved this time she got to spend alone with her mother. Her older sister, Carol, always preferred to stay inside the air conditioning with their grandmother and watch *Love of Life* and *The Doctors*.

As they had waited for cars to pass, Kate looked at one of those gigantic oaks that dotted the coastline. Her grandfather had recently told her you could tell a tree's age by counting the rings in its trunk after cutting it.

"How old do you think this tree is? Older than you?" Kate had asked.

Her mother laughed.

"Much older than me," her mother replied. "This tree started growing long before I came into this world and it will probably be here long after we're all gone."

Kate's tiny five-year-old hand wiped the summer sweat from her brow. She couldn't even begin to fathom a period of time much older than her mother and long after her life.

Many years later, when Kate saw the coastline after Hurricane Katrina, her eyes immediately filled with tears over the damage or complete disappearance of various parts of her hometown. When she saw the oaks, many of which had been reduced to jagged trunks or simply killed by saltwater from the storm surges, she felt an even greater sense of loss.

After a good amount of time had passed, sculptors came into town and with saws, varnish, and other tools turned the trunks of those trees from signs of destruction and trauma into beautiful pieces of artwork celebrating the Mississippi Coast and its culture. Trunks turned into seagulls and other symbols of coastal life.

It had been this transformation that first convinced Kate that beauty could sometimes arise from the worst of nightmares.

Chapter 1- *October 2006*

Javier chuckled as he looked up into the bright moonlit sky and saw a bat fly between two pine trees. He and Alison had cuddled up earlier that evening on a blanket underneath a star-drenched sky, surrounded by half-constructed houses. She laughed at his disbelief when she told him that what flew overhead had not been a bird.

"Yeah, a bat, city boy. You do know what a bat is, right?" she said teasingly.

"Of course I know what a bat is. I just didn't expect them to be flying around at night here in Mississippi. I thought they lived in, you know, caves and drank blood," Javier said, wrapping his arms tighter around her. Her warm breath against his neck stirred the river of testosterone that churned through his veins every time she came within twenty feet of him.

"These aren't the blood-sucking bats," she whispered in his ear. "They just eat bugs."

"Good to know," he said.

"The first few nights after the storm," Alison began, "sometimes I would just lay outside in the backyard looking up at the stars, wondering how all of this could have happened to so many people I care about."

"I'm sorry you had to go through all that," Javier said before gathering her into a deep kiss.

Javier was jolted back to the present when a blast of chilly wind blew through him. He stuffed his hands into his jacket pockets. He had never been in temperatures below the 40s before he moved here. He could even see his breath under the moonlight.

He checked his watch and saw that it was still a few minutes early. She'd be here, and tomorrow they wouldn't have to hide anything any more.

Alison pulled her cheerleading jacket tighter around her body as she quietly walked through the kitchen and out the backdoor. She had waited impatiently at the top of the stairs for the sounds that would confirm that her parents had gone to bed – two flushes of the toilet in the bathroom connected to their bedroom, her father loudly asking if her mother had set the alarm even though her mother never, ever, forgot and, finally, the slamming of their bedroom door.

Tonight it felt like her parents had taken forever to settle down, but Alison had learned at the young age of fourteen when she tried to sneak out to her friend Missy's house after curfew one night. She hadn't even thought of attempting to sneak out until they had gone to bed. Her parents had grounded her a month over the Missy incident. Always so over-protective. Always, Alison thought.

She glanced at the time on her cell phone and saw that she still had a few minutes. Tonight, she wanted to spend every moment she could with Javier. He had been all she could think about as she stood on the sidelines of the football field and cheered with her squad. She'd been so out of it she almost forgot to catch Missy with Madison Ashcroft after they finished a pyramid. Madison had given Alison a dirty look when they caught Missy. Madison could tell that Alison had almost forgotten, and if one thing pissed off Madison Ashcroft more than anything else, it was for one of her cheers to get screwed up. Alison always thought Madison took cheering way too seriously. After all, they weren't curing cancer, for God's sake.

When she started down the driveway, she was startled to see her mother standing under the oak tree next to the house. Their eyes met and Alison was not only surprised to see her mother outside in the yard, but was even more surprised to see that her Mother looked like she had been caught in the middle of an indecent act.

"Mom?" Alison said.

Beverly wiped her hands on her pants and tried to regain her composure.

"What are you doing out here, young lady? Shouldn't you be in bed?"

"Shouldn't you?" Alison asked, in a moment of new-found bravery.

Surprisingly, her mother seemed at a loss for words as she started walking back towards the house.

"I thought I heard something outside," Beverly said, in a feeble attempt at an excuse.

As she walked closer, Alison could see that her mother looked visibly upset.

"Mom, are you okay?" she asked, now feeling genuinely concerned.

"Yeah, of course," Beverly said. "And where were you going?"

"I, uh, was going to Missy's to get my notes for the test on Monday. I forgot them," Alison said, ready to bear her mother's wrath.

Beverly took a deep breath and wrapped her arms around her chest.

"Well…" she said, not looking convinced at all. "Don't be out too late, okay?"

"Oh…okay," Alison said, taken aback by this unexpected permission. She started to walk back down the driveway to the Ford Mustang her father had given her on her sixteenth birthday, but she stopped and turned back to look at her mother, who still stood in the carport. "Mom, are you sure you're okay?"

"Sure," Beverly said. "Be careful, Alison."

Alison nodded and headed to her car.

"I told you not to eat Mexican food before bed, Robert," Kate said, shaking her head as she drank her herbal tea.

"Yes, Kate, I remember," Robert said, searching through the cabinets for an antacid.

"You should have a light supper before bed. Not those spicy tacos from that drive-thru place."

"Yes, Kate," he said, sarcastically. "I'll make sure and run all future food ingestion by ya, okay? Now could you help me find the damn Mylanta."

"Second cupboard on the left at the top," she answered, obviously knowing all along.

"Thanks," Robert said dryly.

"Robert," she said, brushing back a few strands of the baby blonde shade of hair that had covered her gray for fifteen years already. "I'm worried about you. That you're taking on too much. We're pushing fifty. We don't have the energy we used to in our thirties."

"I'm fine," Robert insisted, before drinking the Mylanta straight from the bottle.

"It's just that Sandy's husband. . ." Kate began before looking away.

Robert sighed loudly.

"That's not going to happen to me. I'm not going to have a heart attack," he replied, suddenly sounding softer. "We finish this project and we're set, Katherine. Set for the rest of our lives, probably."

Kate walked around the counter and hugged her husband.

"I know. I just worry. I can't help it. I worry about us, Matt, and Sean."

"Everyone is just fine."

The kitchen door slammed shut, and Matt, their seventeen-year-old, came stomping in the house.

"Hey, son. How are you?" Robert said.

"Okay," Matt muttered under his breath.

"You want some...?" Kate started to say, but before she could offer her son any of the pound cake she had made earlier that evening, he had already stormed out of the room, and she could hear his quick footsteps bounding up the stairs.

Sean allowed Caleb to hold him even tighter despite the fact that he felt warm. Caleb was a big cuddler, and immediately after making love, he'd snuggle as close as he could to Sean and immediately fall asleep. Sean, feeling more awake than ever, would often just lay there listening to his boyfriend's soft snores and the sounds drifting in from Market Street in San Francisco.

Sometimes, during these moments, he would watch Caleb sleep and wonder why in God's name this sweet, cute guy seemed to want to be a part of his life so much. Caleb had always been so giving, loving, and more romantic than any guy in his life before had ever been. In fact, none of them acted as if they cared one iota about romance as long as the sex came their way.

Yet Sean knew that he had still not fully begun to open up to Caleb and really let him into his life. He felt as though he had tried, but he knew that he still held back. He also knew that Caleb sensed it, and Sean couldn't help but wonder how much longer Caleb would stick around.

Suddenly, Caleb's eyes fluttered open, and he looked at Sean and smiled.

"I'm sorry I fell asleep," he said.

Sean kissed his forehead.

"It's okay," he said. "I like watching you sleep."

Caleb smiled.

At that moment, Sean felt a wave of uneasiness shoot through his body, and it had nothing to do with Caleb.

"Everything okay?" Caleb asked, looking worried.

"Yeah. Just got a weird feeling all of a sudden. I'm sure it's nothing."

***

"Hey, you," Alison said, walking up behind Javier and wrapping her arms around him.

Javier, smiling, turned around, picked her up in his arms, and kissed her deeply.

"Come on," Alison said, grabbing his hand and leading him down the street.

Surrounding them on both sides were rows of what would eventually be high-end houses, replacing the houses the high winds and waters had swept away. Some weren't much more than a shell while others would be completed within a matter of a month or so. It had struck Alison as weird more than once that the quiet place that she and Javier had had their secret nighttime encounters, the place their romance had blossomed, would soon be a bustling new neighborhood development. Just a year ago, it had been a thriving middle class neighborhood. Children would ride their bicycles down the street, fathers would water their new lawns, and neighborhood mothers would arrange play dates for their children.

Every square inch of the new development had been carefully planned by Matt's father and then gradually brought into being by Javier's father in the new post-Hurricane Katrina world of Southern Mississippi, a moment in time where many suffered and some, like Matt's father, profited from the new real estate boom.

They headed to a huge two-story home that had just been framed in…the perfect hiding place for two young lovers.

"After tonight…" Alison said.

"We're going to be together. No matter what they say," Javier answered.

"Unless," Alison giggled, "we just want some extra privacy."

Matt quietly closed the door of his father's upstairs study. His father hated anyone else going into the study.

"This is my domain, my sanctuary," Robert often told his family.

And when his father went inside and shut the door behind him, not even Matt's mother dared to disturb him. What his father did in there, really, no one knew. Matt wasn't sure he even wanted to know.

When his parents went on vacation to Memphis earlier in the year, curiosity got the best of Matt, and he snuck into the room and began to explore – carefully. He looked through what turned out to be nothing more than boring business documents and carefully replaced each one in the exact spot it had been. He found a bag of chewing tobacco, a surprise since he had never seen his father chew it before.

What was hidden in the second from the bottom drawer on the right side surprised him the most. There, carefully hidden behind pieces of his father's high school mementos – yearbooks and his old jersey – was a small pistol. Matt never knew his father even owned a gun. That day he had picked the gun up carefully, admiring its weight for such a small object and the surge of power he had felt holding it. From that moment, the idea of the gun never left his mind. He thought about it and what could be done with a firearm often.

Now the time had come for him to put it to use.

Matt quickly but quietly opened the same drawer now, reached in the back, and pulled out the gun.

Chapter 2- *August 2006*

Enrique stared at the stretch of expansive Texas desert before him and wiped the sweat from his forehead with a paper napkin. Besides the tiny ramshackle gas station behind him, there were no other buildings in sight. Only orange-red dirt, a paved highway, and endless cactuses and small shrubs dotted the landscape.

He felt vaguely nauseous, and he couldn't be sure if the lack of lunch or the unforgiving heat was the cause. Maybe he should have had his wife buy him a ginger ale inside the store. If they had ginger ale out here, that is.

He leaned back against his family's silver Toyota Camry and sighed. What could possibly be taking his family so long? Eager to get back on the road and, hopefully, meet the movers at their new home, Enrique wanted to get started. The sooner he could start, and make this work, the sooner he could prove the naysayers, including his in-laws, wrong. His forty-one years of life had taught him one thing: the only way to get anywhere in life was to take risks – sometimes big ones.

He could see his wife, Carmen, inside the store trying to gear the kids towards the healthier snacks rather than the chocolate, chips, and soda they usually gravitated towards. Her unshakeable faith in him kept him going during the times he doubted himself.

From the moment they met as teens outside a convenience store in East L.A., him hanging out with his cousins trying to figure out how they could get some cigarettes and her with her girlfriends buying sodas after school, she had this blind faith in him that he thought both remarkable and mystifying at the same time.

Her parents hadn't crossed the Mexican border on foot like his had. In fact, her family had been living in California when it was part of Mexico. Despite his skin having the same exact skin shade as Carmen's, her parents considered him unacceptable as a match for their daughter. Her parents were both teachers, and they pushed their daughter to focus on her education. His parents both worked in a clothing factory – his mother a seamstress and his father a box packer. They both pushed their son to get a job and help the family with money. Education was seen as a luxury for the rich. It had been Carmen who somehow convinced him of the merits of an education and supported him when it came to getting a college education when no one else did.

She even managed to keep their three restless kids in line and from arguing, for the most part, during this cross-country drive.

Javier, the oldest at seventeen, hadn't said much from the moment the move was announced over a family dinner. He didn't need to. His face said it all. Enrique could see the doubt in his son's eyes.

Their daughter, Adriana, almost fifteen, had been more than vocal about leaving Los Angeles for Long Beach, a small Mississippi town. In short, she thought he was crazy. She screamed, cried, and threw her head on the dinner table.

"Why are you doing this to us?" she pleaded.

"I'm doing this for us," Enrique had stressed.

The rest of the family had just stared down at their dinner plates.

"And the year before my *quinceañera*! No one there will even know what the hell a *quinceañera* is," Adriana sobbed, her face flushed with anger.

"Adriana, do not speak to your father that way," Carmen scolded.

There were a few moments of awkward silence around the dinner table. No one ate. They just stared at their laps. Until little
Ever, age nine, finally broke the silence.

"Sounds like fun to me, *Papi*," he said, in a small little voice.
"I'd like to see some place new."

Enrique had reached over and patted his son on the head.

Carmen's hand on his shoulder brought Enrique back to the
future, the uncertainty and the blistering desert heat.

Their eyes met, and she smiled.

"We're making good time, huh?" she said reassuringly.

"Hope so," Enrique said.

He turned around and saw his children walking out of the
store.

"Come on," Carmen said, gently grabbing his hand. "The
sooner we get to Mississippi, the sooner I can unpack these boxes
and start making a home."

"Robert, are you really sure about this hire?" Kate asked, as she sat
across from his work desk sorting through the day's mail.

The two had worked together in Robert's real estate development business ever since Matt began elementary school. Before
that, Robert had long complained of the hard time he had finding a
secretary who he felt could do a good job, someone that would
"get him." When Kate announced that she wanted the job, Robert
had been initially hesitant. He worried that working together might
equal *too much* togetherness. After some insistence on Kate's part,
Robert had agreed to give it a two-week trial. She'd been his right
hand at work for years now. She had impressed him over the years
with her business savvy. And she loved to play the Devil's advo-
cate.

Robert reached for his third cup of coffee that morning and
yawned. He had been up most of the night with heartburn. Damn
peppers!

"I'm telling you," he began, "this guy comes highly recommended from a good friend. He says Enrique is a real go-getter,

and we need someone who's bilingual. He can reach these workers in ways we just can't."

Ever since Hurricane Katrina, there had been a flood of Latino immigrants into their small Mississippi coastal town, Long Beach. Many had shown up after word spread there would be a lot of construction jobs since not only the town, but the surrounding area had almost been wiped off the map, with ninety percent of coast-line buildings being destroyed.

Since the workforce had been so depleted by the hurricane, they were warmly welcomed – at least by the employers. The workers tended to be dedicated and worked for cheap. The only problem was the language barrier since most of them spoke limited English. That's when Robert knew that if he wanted to stay ahead of the post-Katrina construction boom, he had to find a supervisor who was bilingual.

"It's just so strange here now. So many….different people," Kate said, her voice trailing off.

"And the perfect time…to make some money," Robert said.

"Alison! Don! Breakfast is ready!" Alison heard her mother, Beverly, scream up the stairs.

Every morning, despite the fact that she didn't have a set schedule, Beverly would get up at six a.m. to see her husband off to work and her daughter to school. As the years went on, though, Alison felt like her mother was just getting in their way in the mornings. Alison knew her mother thought that's what any good wife and mother would do – see her family off.

Alison could hear her mother scrambling eggs. They were always firm. Just like Alison liked them. She then heard her pop four pieces of bread into the toaster.

Alison walked into the kitchen with her father, Don, a lawyer, who wore a dark navy three-piece suit and carrying a briefcase.

"The toast is almost ready," Beverly said.

"Oh," Don said, looking distracted as he went through some mail on the table. "Sorry, hon. I gotta run, or I'm going to be late for a meeting."

"Well, at least have some…" Beverly started to say.

"I'll grab something later this morning. I may be late for dinner, too," he said, briefly stopping to place a chaste kiss on Beverly's cheek. "See you later."

And with that, he practically ran out the kitchen door. Almost immediately, Alison could hear him cranking his Escalade.

Alison slung her book bag over her shoulder and tried to put her dark blonde hair into a ponytail.

"Scrambled eggs! Extra firm!" Beverly said, scooping a helping of eggs on the plate.

"Sorry, mom. I gotta go or I'm going to be late for practice."

"But…" Beverly started to protest.

Too late. Alison started out the door and simultaneously heard the darkened toast pop up out of the toaster.

Alison glanced back and through the kitchen window to see her mother reach into the kitchen drawer, pull out a fork, and eat some of the eggs straight from the frying pan.

Sean sat in his cubicle and stared at the wall calendar thumb-tacked above his head. A date he was thoroughly dreading stared back at him, circled in bright, doom-laden red. He could feel his stomach begin to ache just thinking about that day.

"Could you run the report for me on last June's donations?" his boss, T.J., asked as he popped his head into Sean's cubby.

"Huh?" Sean tried to snap his mind back to the present.

"Miss Thing," T.J., said, moaning. "Hello! Wake up! I need the report on donations for June."

"Oh, yeah, sure," Sean answered. He began to open a program on his computer.

Sean had worked at the San Francisco AIDS Wellness Initiative for two years now. He had hightailed it to San Francisco with all of his savings right after graduating from the University of Southern Mississippi with a degree in Marketing. After working a series of crazy temp jobs, he finally landed the gig as an office manager with the Initiative. He didn't find his daily tasks all that exciting, but the job was paying the bills, and T.J. had become a great friend and mentor.

"Where's your mind at this morning?" T.J. asked.

"Just thinking about going home for my dad's birthday. God, I dread it. I have nothing in common with anyone there, and I don't think my dad would miss me one second if I wasn't there," Sean said.

"That can't be true."

"It is. I might as well be invisible, especially with my little brother the straight jock extraordinaire hogging the limelight. I'll just have to sit around and watch my parents fawn over him. I don't know how I let myself commit to going."

T.J. cocked an eyebrow. "Maybe because deep down you actually want to be there."

Sean just grunted and said, "I'll have the report for you in fifteen."

Thanks," T.J. said. "And isn't this evening your first night of volunteer work at the Gay and Lesbian Center?"

"Yep," Sean answered, running his fingers through his reddish brown hair.

"About time you were getting out and meeting some people," T.J. said, smiling.

Sean smiled back, but his mind kept wandering between the reports he needed to run and his last trip back home.

On August 30, 2005, Sean thought he might officially lose his mind. He sat in front of the television watching the continuous coverage of the aftermath of Hurricane Katrina.

Fortunately, or unfortunately, the office was being renovated, and T.J. had Sean working from home. Not that Sean could get anything accomplished. He couldn't peel his eyes away from the TV and its images of floods, fires, death, and destruction.

He had never felt so helpless as he had the past couple of days. The phone lines all along the Mississippi coast had been out for a while now. He had no way of contacting his family to find out if they were okay.

The last conversation he had had with his mother had been two days earlier.

"Are you sure you guys shouldn't evacuate?" Sean had said to her, while he watched the great swirl of a storm on the Weather Channel's satellite radar.

"You know how your dad is. He keeps saying he's been through worse storms than this," Kate said, barely able to hide the concern in her voice. "You know how the weather people are anyway. They love to make a big deal out of things. It gets more people to watch the news."

"I don't know, Mom. This storm looks huge. Look at what it's already done in Florida. If it looks like it may get out of hand, promise me you guys will get the hell out of there," Sean had pleaded.

"Promise," Kate said, not sounding all that convincing. "I better head to the store before all the bread and milk are gone."

"I love you," Sean said, a sense of urgency in his voice.

"Love you, too," Kate had said.

Every few hours, Sean had to force himself to leave his apartment to take a walk, go to the supermarket, something, anything. But when he did, he couldn't help but notice how the San Francisco world was going about its business. People were going to work, shopping, sitting at cafes, chatting, as though nothing out of the ordinary had happened.

Sometimes he'd overhear someone say something like, "Can you believe what's happening in New Orleans?"

No one mentioned Mississippi and the vast destruction that had taken place there. The national news had barely even skimmed the surface, but from what Sean could see on the TV or read on the net, the damage had been massive.

Did my family get out in time? If they stayed in their house on the edge of the Coast, what had become of them? The thoughts played over and over in his head.

T.J. would call periodically to check on him, and insisted that he come over for dinner that night.

"There's no way I'm going to let you sit in that apartment alone right now," T.J. said. "Be here at six."

But that left hours for Sean to obsess in front of the television and to think the worse.

When Eric, a guy he dated, called and asked how he was and did he want to go to lunch, Sean felt a huge wave of relief.

T.J. would have flipped if he knew Sean was going to lunch with Eric.

"That boy is toxic to you, Sean," T.J. had said recently, one night over drinks after Sean had confessed how much he still thought about Eric and how what he had felt for him had been so different than for other guys.

"I think we just met at the wrong time," Sean said. "If it had been another time…"

"The same thing would have happened," T.J. said. "The guy's a self-obsessed flake. He only wants you when he doesn't have you."

Sean knew deep down that T.J. was probably right, but he didn't want to believe it. It felt better to romanticize what they had had even if it hurt his heart.

But Sean hadn't thought twice when Eric asked him out to lunch. It was just a concerned friend thing on Eric's part, Sean told himself. It'd be nice not to be alone for a while. Anything to distract him was welcomed.

He met Eric, clad in jeans and gray Gap pullover, out in front of his apartment building. The morning fog from the San Francisco Bay had still not completely cleared out for the day and a chill still clung to the air. It made Sean think about the humidity back home and how suffocating it must feel there without any air conditioning and with the stench of death drifting through the wind.

"Hey, mister," Eric said, walking up to him, all smiles.

He gave Sean a tight, hug which felt so good. It felt good just to be hugged by anyone since he felt he could break down and start crying at any second.

"Thanks for taking me to lunch," Sean said.

"Yeah, I've been thinking about you. How's your family?"

"Still haven't heard anything."

Eric shook his head. "Sorry about that."

Sean and Eric's brief bursts at courtship had always felt intense for Sean, with a strong rush of feelings, longing, and wanting to be near him. Eric, having traveled extensively as part of his graduate studies in environmental science, seemed much more worldly to Sean, who had basically been to only two places: back home and Northern California. Eric's couple of extra years in age also gave him an aura of further developed maturity. Somehow, Sean had always managed to gloss over Eric's hot and cold behavior when it came to him. He had never felt like he knew where he stood with Eric when they had dated, as if he thought Eric always had an eye out just in case someone slightly better came along.

"We're going to go grab some burgers," Eric announced. "Come on."

Sean thought for a brief second that it would have been nice if Eric had asked him if he wanted burgers, but Sean told himself he didn't care. He was just happy to be out of the house and with someone else.

At Slider's in the Castro, Eric and Sean ordered their burgers and sat at a table in the back. Above them, a TV played news coverage from New Orleans. Sean tried as best he could not to look.

"How's everything else going?" Eric asked, between bites of his burger.

Sean's food sat in front of him, untouched. The thought of any food right now made him slightly nauseous.

"Just been busy with work," he said.

A couple of moments passed, and then Eric said, "There's something I need to tell you."

Sean glanced up for a second at the TV and images of people on roofs waving for help. Did his parent's house make it?

"What's up?" he asked, trying to focus on what Eric was saying.

"I'm seeing someone new," Eric said.

"Oh," Sean said. "Okay. Good for you."

Why did Eric have to bring this up now, for God's sake? As if he didn't have enough on his mind.

"For about six weeks now," Eric said.

Sean absent-mindedly moved some fries around on his plate. "Cool," he said quietly. "How's it going?"

"Good. We're buying a loft together." Eric was casual.

Sean dropped a French fry that had almost made it to his mouth.

"You're buying a loft with someone you just met six weeks ago?" he asked, stunned.

"Yeah, I know. Some of my friends think I'm nuts for moving so fast. It just feels right. You know?"

Sean had never even been able to get Eric to use the term boy-friend, and now here he was moving in with someone he had practically just met. Why this guy? Why now?

"Wow, that's…amazing," he said, for lack of thinking of anything better.

"I just wanted you to know," Eric said, pushing his empty plate to the side. "How do you feel about that?"

"What do you mean?" Sean said. "You want to know how I feel about what?"

"Well, I just want to make sure that if we're friends I can talk to you about these things. How do you feel about this?"

Sean thought about it for a couple of seconds, and then he decided he wanted to tell Eric he thought he was a self-involved asshole. He wanted to remind Eric that he didn't even know if his family was dead or alive, as they sat in this diner having lunch. He felt like telling him that he couldn't give a flying fuck if Eric wanted to marry a house fern. He felt like yelling at him about how clueless Eric could be that he thought whatever news he had about his new "boyfriend" trumped the fact that his family could be hurt…or even worse.

But instead, he said, "I'm happy for you. I need to get back home to do some work. Thanks for lunch."

It simply amazed him that in those few minutes, the thoughts he had carried for so long about what could have been or what

might have been between Eric and himself had evaporated completely. Clarity in his mind on what the situation had been all along
took over. That's the thing about horrible tragedies. They sometimes put things in perspective, in a quick, blow-to-the-head sort of
way.

When he flew home that first Christmas after Katrina, the first
thing he noticed as the plane began its descent into the Gulfport-
Biloxi Regional Airport was the expanse of bright blue he could see
when he looked out of the plane's window. Many of the houses
that remained had lost their roofs, and now those houses were
covered by tarps creating a great bright blue sea visible from the
air.

He felt so nervous about returning home for the first time
since the storm. Guilt at having not been there to help out had
gnawed at his conscience and seeped into his soul. As much as he
knew he didn't belong in Mississippi anymore, it was still home,
and he felt an obligation to Long Beach, to the entire Coast.

Before he had left for college in San Francisco, Emma, his maternal grandmother, had told him over lemonade and tea cookies,
"That's all right, sweetness. You go do what you have to do." She
leaned over the kitchen table and placed her hand on top of his.
"You'll always be a Southerner, you know? It doesn't matter how
long you're gone for or what happens in the meantime, the South is
in you, part of you. And it will always beckon you home at times.
The roots of your family are as intertwined and deep with this land
as those of a Mississippi pine tree. Don't forget that."

His mother, minus his father and brother, met him outside the
airport. She smiled at him reassuringly, but Sean could sense this
was no easy task for his mother.

"Welcome home! Merry Christmas!" Kate had said, opening
her arms.

Sean hugged her and held her for a moment longer than usual,
so relieved to see her in person and in good health.

"Merry Christmas," he replied.

"Your dad and Matt went hunting with your dad's cousins. You know how those two are about deer season," Kate said.

"I know," Sean said, hurt but not allowing it to show. Deer season had overshadowed his return home.

"They'll be back for dinner," Kate said, standing back a foot and gazing at her son. "You sure are a sight for sore eyes."

Sean sat his suitcase down next to him to give his arm a rest and said, "It's good to see you, too."

"Where would you like to go first?" she asked.

"I want to go to the house, Mom."

Kate shook her head, unsure. "The new house isn't ready yet, honey. You know we're still staying at the condo in Diamondhead. Right next to the golf course. Your dad has been in golf heaven. What he gets out of knocking that little ball around I'll never know."

"No, Mom, I mean our house, where we lived. I want to see it."

Kate hesitated for a moment and bit her lower lip, as she often did while in deep thought.

"Are you sure that's the first thing you want to see, honey?" she asked. "It's a lot to take in if you haven't seen it."

"I'm sure. I need to see it," he insisted.

Kate nodded silently and began to head towards the car. Sean picked up his bag and followed.

As they drove down Highway 49 towards Beach Boulevard, Sean sat in silence taking in all of the destruction around him. Many strip malls, houses and apartment buildings remained as nothing but mere shells of their former selves, just skeleton buildings with no walls or windows.

"They just opened part of the boulevard back up for traffic this week," Kate said.

Sean wondered how seeing all of this every day, not to mention what his family had gone through during and the weeks after the storm, had affected his mother. He wondered how it had affected his entire family and what his mother really felt under the façade of a cheery Christmas smile.

A few days after the storm, Sean had finally received a telephone call from Kate telling him that they were all right. They had stayed and ended up getting rescued by boat during the storm surges. Matt had been the last one to get out of the house. He asked her how the house was after the storm. His mother had grimly told him the house was simply gone now, and they had evacuated to his Aunt Carol's in Laurel for the meantime.

Sean sat in shock as they drove through what used to be his family's neighborhood. Large grand homes, some over two hundred years old, had vanished. In their place were piles of rubble, random objects such as an office chair or the remains of a kitchen table, and the occasional FEMA trailer.

Kate pulled up into the driveway of the lot where their two-story home had once stood and said, "That's all there is now."

Silently, Sean got out of the car followed by his mother. Even though he didn't have many happy memories growing up in his parent's house, the fact that the home had completely disappeared sent shivers through his body. All that remained were the front steps and the concrete slab the house had sat on. Soon there would be a new home for his family, one in which he had never lived or had any memories of.

"Jesus Christ," he muttered.

He noticed some clothes, pots, and even a mattress caught up in some decaying trees.

"I know, I know," Kate said quietly.

Sean walked over and put his arm around his mother. He tried to come up with something to say, but he didn't think anything he could think of would do justice to the moment.

Sean took a deep breath and tried to get himself to focus on the spreadsheet on his computer's display screen.

"Reports!" he heard T.J.'s voice boom from the back of the office.

"Coming!" Sean called back.

As with everything else in his life, he'd suck it up and find the strength to get through this latest trip back home.

Inside the school gym, Matt and his friend, Beau, sat on the bleachers and watched the cheerleaders practice a new routine, which included their most elaborate pyramid yet, for the school year's first pep rally. Their eyes lingered leisurely on the young women, thoughts of sweat and sex dominating their minds as they do for any teenaged boy.

"Ready! Okay!" Madison, the head cheerleader, chanted loudly while the team dutifully obeyed her commands. "Pirates! Fight! Fight!"

"Now that's a hot piece of ass," Beau muttered, as they watched Missy McDonough climb to the top of the cheerleading pyramid.

"You can say that again," Matt said, his eyes roaming over Missy's body.

"Hey, man, you already got a hot piece!"

"That don't mean I can't look. And what? You been checking out my girl?" Matt said, feigning anger towards his best friend.

"Man, whatever," Beau said, snickering. "Besides, it's senior year. What you and Alison goin' to do after graduation? Maybe now's the time for you to start seriously playing the field, bro."

"Ain't nothin' goin to happen with Alison and me."

"Pussy whipped," Beau muttered under his breath.

"Man, shut the hell up," Matt said, elbowing his friend. "You don't know what you're talking about."

"Um, hmm."

Matt and Beau were the stars of the football team, the Pirates. Matt had a true linebacker's build – stocky and muscular. His dark hair and blue eyes caught the eyes of many of the girls on campus, but so far, Sean only had eyes for Alison. They'd been dating since sophomore year. She was definitely his girl. Beau, on the other hand, had the reputation for being a player. African-American, standing at 6'2", 185 pounds, lean muscle, and a bright smile, Beau turned plenty of heads, too. There'd been a few girls that tried to pursue him for the long haul, but he wouldn't have it. "This is too good not to spread around," Beau had once told Matt.

Matt watched from the bleachers as Alison tried to support two of her fellow cheerleaders who stood on her shoulders.

"When they're done with practice, want to see if Alison…and maybe Missy want to go to the beach?" Matt asked.

"Hell, yeah," Beau said. "Especially if Missy is going to wear that fucking hot little red bikini. Damn, got to readjust my pants just thinking about it."

"Hi, I'm Caleb, the volunteer coordinator here at the Center," a twenty-something-year-old with dark hair and killer green eyes that begged to be gazed into said to Sean, and shook his hand.

Sean immediately felt the fabled butterflies in his stomach start to swarm. A couple of moments went by as he just stared at the guy. Then, embarrassed, he realized Caleb was waiting for some sort of reply.

"Oh, uh…nice to meet you. I'm Sean."

Caleb smiled.

"Is that a slight Southern accent I detect?"

"Probably. I'm originally from Mississippi," Sean said.

Sometimes he liked it when people pointed out his accent because it made him feel special. Sometimes, though, he resented it because it made him feel different.

"Well, it's very charming," Caleb said. "Follow me."

He led Sean down a long winding hallway with cubicles on one side and meeting rooms on the other.

"What made you decide to volunteer for the Gay & Lesbian Center?" Caleb asked as he led the way.

"You know, giving back more to the community and stuff," Sean answered.

"No community service hours to complete?" Caleb raised an eyebrow. "It's cool if that's why you're here."

"Nope. Here out of my own free will."

"Very cool," Caleb said, nodding his head.

Sean got the impression that perhaps there weren't many others who volunteered time for the good deed aspect.

Caleb opened the door to a huge entryway and motioned for Sean to walk on inside.

He walked in to find the space from floor to ceiling filled with books on practically every gay subject he could think of: from lesbian pulp fiction to gay self-help to erotica and more. Nothing appeared in order. Some books sat in clumps on the floor.

"Wow!" he said feeling a little overwhelmed. Was his job to organize this mess?

Caleb chuckled.

"Welcome to our library in progress. As you can see it needs a little work. Just getting things categorized would be a great start. Hell, just getting the fiction on one side and the non-fiction on the other would be a great start."

Sean's eyes widened as he walked along the tiny pathway around the room and surveyed the contents.

"A lot here, huh?" Sean commented.

"Don't let it intimidate you," Caleb said, patting Sean's back and shooting a little electrical charge through his body. "Just take it one thing at a time. Due to budget cuts, we haven't had anybody work on this in over two years. I'm sure you're man enough to handle it. I have a good feeling about you, Southern Boy."

Caleb winked at him, turned around, and left Sean with the mountain of books.

Sean's eyes glazed over as his eyes roamed around the room. Maybe this giving back to the community thing wouldn't be as much fun as he thought. But he had to admit, Caleb was pretty damn cute.

The summer heat beat down on the white sand along the beach with the earliest hint of fall's arrival nowhere in sight. Alison and Matt walked hand in hand, each carrying their shoes with their other, the damp sand squishing beneath their toes. Beau and Missy followed behind them with Beau trying to chase Missy, squealing, into the tide as it came in.

Much to Beau's disappointment, Missy had insisted that she didn't have time to go home and get a swimsuit before she had to meet her parents for dinner. So the four decided to take a walk along the beach instead. Automatically, they kept their gaze towards the water and sand and not the destruction on the other side.

"You're being quiet this afternoon," Alison said, squeezing Matt's hand. She could always tell when something deep was on his mind, whether he told her what it was or not.

"Just thinking about senior year. Finally here," Matt said.

"Finally, we'll rule the school!" Alison exclaimed.

"Yeah, finally," Matt muttered.

They could hear Missy and Beau laughing and still chasing each other. Matt wished he could somehow freeze this moment in time; that things could remain this way always.

"My dad really wants me to go to Ole Miss to play ball," Matt said.

"Yeah, I always thought that was the plan anyway. It's what you want, right?" Alison asked.

"What do you want?" he asked.

"Guys, I gotta start walking back to the car!" Missy called out. "My mom's going to kill me if I'm late again for dinner."

"Okay!" Alison called back.

She led Matt back towards the car, and he noticed that she had not answered.

As they drove down Beach Boulevard along the Mississippi Gulf Coast, Enrique and his family were speechless. Sure, they had all seen on the news the destruction caused by Hurricane Katrina on the television right after it had happened. But it had been over a year, hadn't it?

"My Lord," Carmen said, crossing her chest in prayer.

Most of the beach-front property looked as if a giant had simply taken a hand and wiped away all the buildings, street signs, and landmarks along the way. One block after the next, the family saw concrete steps that led to nowhere, an eerie reminder of all the grand homes that must have dotted the shoreline. A few commercial signs still stood and were the only evidence that strip malls had once been in place.

"Looks like a bomb went off here," Adriana said, staring out the window.

"It probably felt like it, too, *mija*,"

Javier quietly wondered to himself if his father really had an idea of where he was bringing them. The place looked like a war zone. Why would anyone want to live here?

"Ever, remember the pictures I showed you of what it looked like before we left?" Enrique asked the kids.

"There were all these really big houses and old trees!" Ever exclaimed.

"Yep, some of those houses were here for over 200 years. They'd survived hurricanes but not this one," Enrique said.

"Wow," Javier managed to say. All he could think about was how depressing it all looked. As if being taken away from the only world he had ever known in his senior year wasn't enough, living here would be one big downer.

"That's why we're here," Enrique said. "To help these people rebuild. We're going to help make it even better than before."

Javier wondered if this was even possible. He tried to imagine what the place had looked like before, but not enough evidence remained to give him much of a clue.

"Where are the street signs for God sake?" Enrique asked aloud to no one in particular. He kept glancing down at a map in his lap.

"Look!" Carmen said, pointing to some people walking along the beach and playing around as if nothing bad had happened. "There're some kids on the beach."

Javier noticed a couple of guys and girls that looked around his age. Would he be able to make friends here?

"Can I build a sandcastle this weekend?" Ever asked.

"Maybe, *papito*. We'll see how much unpacking we get done," Enrique answered.

"I think this is it."

Enrique finally took a left turn, heading away from the water, but as they drove inland only more and more devastation appeared.

"Ugh!" Adriana moaned.

"Adriana, don't start!" Carmen commanded.

The family drove in silence for a few minutes, but Javier knew what they were all thinking. How could they possibly live here? Why did they ever leave L.A.? Even though his father had been insistent on his decision, Javier could see the doubt behind his father's eyes.

Finally, they began to pass some commercial property, a couple of gas stations, fast food, and small shopping centers.

"I'll have to find a supermarket first thing, and cook us all a fine meal. That'll be good after all of this diner food along the way, huh? I think I remember what box the pots are in," Carmen said, but no one appeared interested in responding. They just kept staring out the windows.

Enrique saw a street sign and smiled more out of relief than happiness.

"This is our street!" he exclaimed.

His company had arranged a house for him to rent before they had left. They had even agreed to subsidize the rent due to recent skyrocketing rental costs in the area.

They pulled up to a decent sized brick home with a two-car driveway, a yard with an unkempt flower garden and a tall Magnolia tree that had managed to survive the storm.

"Look how big the yard is!" Ever enthused.

Look at all that grass cutting, Javier thought, but didn't say.

"We could never afford a house and yard like this back in L.A.," Enrique felt the need to point out. "Looks like we beat the movers."

"Ready to go check out our new home?" Carmen said, turning around and looking at the kids in the backseat.

"I want to see my new room!" Ever said, practically climbing over Javier to get to the car door.

Javier saw his mother reach over and squeeze his father's hand and say to him, "Let's do this."

Chapter 3

"I knew the project would be massive, but seeing it now...it's huge," Enrique said as they walked down one of the freshly-paved winding streets in the upcoming Magnolia and Pines neighborhood.

In the background, the hammering and sawing of the predominantly Mexican work force could be heard.

"Contractors and real estate agents can't keep up with the demand," Robert said, before stopping and pausing in front of an almost-completed two story, four bedroom Victorian replica. "I'm depending on you to help me to finish before these other developers. You know there's a big bonus for you if you can assist me."

"I understand. I worked under a similar timeline on a neighborhood development in Bakersfield."

"Well, you did come highly recommended, Ricky."

"Enrique," he replied with a polite smile on his face. He hated it when others tried to Anglo-Saxonize his name.

"Enrique," Robert repeated. He then looked across a small field and called out, "Juan, come over here! There's someone I want you to meet."

A muscular and tall Latino man walked over while wiping his sweaty hands on his pants.

"Hello," he said, offering his hand to Enrique.

"This is Juan Gonzalez from Fort Worth. He's been one of the leads with the crews here," Robert said. "This is Enrique Santos, the new supervisor."

"Nice to meet you," Enrique said, shaking Juan's hand.

"I'm going to head back to the office," Robert said. "Juan, can you finish showing Mr. Santos around the rest of the site?"

"Sure thing."

"Just head on back to the office when you finish, and we'll look over some plans," Robert said to Enrique before heading off.

As soon as Robert was out of earshot, Juan leaned over and said, "*Chico*, we are glad to see you. Believe me. The *gringos* that run this place have got no idea what's going on."

As Carmen's car slowly pulled up to Beach View High School, Adriana began to complain even louder. Javier just sat up front next to his mother, staring out the window. He didn't say anything, but he knew his mother could still tell when her son was frightened. Earlier in the morning, Ever had practically jumped out of the car and ran to his elementary school excited to see what school in a new place would be all about.

Carmen slowly began to pull into a long line of cars close to a two story red brick building that looked a little bruised but had made it through the wrath of Katrina. A huge hand-painted banner reading, "Welcome Back Pirates!" hung across the entrance.

"Ugh, this is so wrong! I can't believe you did this to us. Making us come to this hick town and now I've got to go to school where I have no friends and you know they're all going to be racist," Adriana cried.

"God, Adriana, stop being so dramatic," Javier said.

Carmen stopped the car and Adriana and Javier looked out the window at kids who poured out of cars and buses and ran to each other.

"Look, you two," Carmen began, trying to put a smile and a positive spin on the situation. "You've got to look at this as a new opportunity to meet some new people, learn some new things. True, some of it might be very different from what you're used to doing and seeing, but that's the world. It's not all like L.A. Just try and have a good day. Please." She paused before adding, "I'll be here at 3:30 to pick you up."

Without saying a word, both Javier and Adriana got out of the car and cautiously walked towards the front door of the school.

Javier looked back at his mother for a split second, and she smiled at him. He knew her well enough to read the worry in her eyes that she tried so hard to conceal.

Javier and Adriana sat alone at a small table in the back of the school cafeteria. Their trays with hamburgers and extra greasy French fries sat in front of them untouched.

Neither felt like eating.

"Okay if I sit here?" asked a guy with the reddest hair Adriana had ever seen.

Adriana shrugged her shoulders.

"It's a free country...I think," she said, sighing.

"Yeah, man, sit," Javier said, trying to make up for his sister's rudeness. "I'm Javier."

"Brent," the guy said, before tearing into his hamburger as though he hadn't eaten in days. "New kids, huh?" he said, mouth half-full.

"How'd you guess?" Adriana smirked.

"We've been getting lots of new kids since the storm. A lot of Mexican kids," Brent said. He carefully squirted every drop out of his ketchup packet.

"Just because we're Latino doesn't mean we're Mexican, you know? Our ancestors could be from Central or South America, or maybe even Cuba or Puerto Rico. My mom's family lived in California when it was part of Mexico," Adriana said, rolling her eyes.

"Sorry, I didn't mean to offend," Brent said, looking uncomfortable.

"Don't listen to my stupid, rude ass sister. Her name is Adriana, by the way," Javier said. "And anyway we are Mexican or at least our ancestors were. You always lived here?"

Adriana reluctantly began to eat a French fry.

"Yep, whole life. Know everybody, almost. At least before the storm, ya know?" Brent said, his focus shifting to the left of them. "You're getting checked out."

"Huh?" Javier asked.

Adriana's eyes began scanning the cafeteria.

"People have been staring at me all day like I just stepped off a spaceship," she said.

"No, your brother is getting checked out in a good way," Brent said.

Javier finally noticed a group of girls all dressed in cheerleading uniforms doing a very bad job of pretending not to be staring at him. He thought he may have recognized one of the girls from the beach, the one with the dirty blonde hair and the hourglass figure. If there's one thing Javier already knew, it was that he had a weakness for girls with hourglass figures.

Across the cafeteria a trio of cheerleaders kept shooting glances in Javier's direction.

"Hello, Enrique Iglesias," Missy said, giggling.

"Don't be so cheesy, Missy. Christ!" Alison said, picking at her chili fries. While the rest of the girls obsessed over every little calorie, Alison ate what she wanted. Luckily, she had been blessed with her mother's metabolism, high enough not to pack on the pounds but slow enough to provide some feminine curves.

"You've got to admit he's pretty freaking hot," Madison, the head cheerleader said. "For a Mexican guy."

"Could you sound any more racist, Madison?" Alison said, shaking her head.

"You know I heard that they're all uncircumcised," Missy said.

"Will you shut up? I'm trying to eat," Alison said.

"I wonder what one of those looks like," Madison said. "I mean, do you have to blow it differently?"

Alison rolled her eyes.

"God, you two," she said. "He is cute. I guess that's his sister with him. They look so much alike."

Missy let out a loud laugh, which turned into a snort, embarrassing her.

"Look, they're stuck with Brent Dipplings. God, Brent's such a wuss," Madison said.

"Do you have to be so catty, Madison?" Alison asked, sighing.

"Meow!" Madison exclaimed, spreading out her perfectly manicured rose pink fingernails.

"Hey, fine ladies," Matt said, sitting down at the table, followed by Beau.

"What you girls laughing about?" Beau asked.

"Talking about that hot new Mexican guy," Madison said.

"Whatever," Matt said, putting his arm around Alison's shoulder in a territorial way.

"Yeah, as if there aren't enough spics in town these days," Beau said, shaking his head.

Alison looked back over at the new guy, and suddenly, she found her eyes meeting his. She started to look away, but she found that if only for a split-second, she couldn't do so.

Chapter 4

"Well, hello," Kate said, opening her front door. "Welcome to our home!"

Music from a live band blared from inside the house. Guests stood in the foyer, dressed in their party finest and drinking glasses of the best champagne that could be bought in the state.

Kate, a vision of elegance in her new cream pants suit from Saks in New Orleans, stepped aside for the entire Santos family to enter her house.

"Thanks so much for having us over," Carmen said, shaking Kate's hand, which displayed an eye-catching ruby and sapphire ring.

"Very nice of you to have us over for Robert's birthday party," Enrique said.

"Of course. Our pleasure," Kate said, turning her attention to the Santos children. "And what a beautiful family you have."

In the car, Carmen had grilled the kids on how to behave at the party. She had to tell Ever not to start running throughout the house, Adriana to try and smile, and Javier to keep an eye on Adriana and Ever. Enrique's boss had insisted that he bring his entire family to the party, and both Carmen and Enrique felt a little anxious about how they would circulate through their new social circle.

"And this is Javier," Carmen said, finishing the introductions of her children.

"And what a handsome young man you are, Javier," Kate said.

"Thank you," Javier answered softly and shyly.

Javier saw Matt descend down the staircase that emptied into the foyer, and when Kate turned and saw her son she motioned him over.

"You must know my son, Matt," she said.

Matt swaggered over with a less than enthusiastic look.

"Hey," Javier said. "Yeah, from school."

Kate not so subtly elbowed her son.

"Matt, why don't you take Matt and Adriana out back where your friends are?" Kate strongly suggested.

"Sure," Matt shrugged, leading the way with Javier and Adriana behind him.

"I don't know why we had to come to this," Adriana said under her breath to her brother.

"We just got to deal with it," Javier answered back.

Matt led the two to the backyard that contained a huge pool, tennis court and barbeque pit.

"Holy shit. Look at this place, Javi," Adriana muttered under her breath.

Matt turned around and motioned to the bar in the back.

"Help yourself to something to drink. I'll be back," he said, not bothering to hide his lack of enthusiasm and then heading back in the house.

"So much for Southern hospitality," Adriana said.

"Might as well get something to drink," Javier replied.

His eyes scanned the crowd in the backyard and almost immediately met Alison's, who sat poolside with Missy.

Sean stood on the sidelines near the pool at his father's birthday party, sipping a Jack and Coke and watching the guests mix and mingle. He knew he should have never come here for this. His father had barely said two words to him since he had arrived the day before. He'd spent most of his time in one of the new guest rooms upstairs, surfing the internet on his laptop and thinking about that volunteer coordinator, Caleb. Sean had barely spoken to him, but for some odd reason he'd been thinking about him ever since. Something about the guy made his heart race with nervous energy.

Honestly, he hated anyone making him feel this way. He felt powerless and irrational when infatuated. So for quite a while he just kept his distance emotionally from any man. The thought of giving his heart away was much too frightening. He hadn't felt this way since Eric.

"I'm so glad you're here, honey," Kate said, putting her hand on Sean's arm.

Sean just smiled. Better not to say anything than something bad.

"Why are you standing in this corner all by yourself?" Kate asked.

"I'm fine. Just relaxing," he answered.

She reached up smoothed down his hair, something she had always done since he was little when she was about to broach a serious topic.

"You know, sweetie, ever since the storm…" she began, but then trailed off for a second. "It just reminds you what's truly important in life. I wish you'd come back home."

"Mother, we've had this discussion before. There's just nothing for me here."

"We're here," Kate protested.

"I have extra considerations in my life. You know that," Sean said, alluding to the fact that he was gay. Even though it was no secret it had not become a topic that his family discussed openly.

"What about New Orleans? You used to love going there, and it's only two hours away."

"New Orleans is a mess right now. Besides, San Francisco is my home," Sean said, feeling anger beginning to rise inside him. "We've had this discussion before, Mother."

"I know, I know."

"Shouldn't you be socializing with all of your guests anyway?" he said, before finishing off his cocktail.

Kate started to speak but then stopped. She leaned over and placed a kiss on her son's cheek.

"Try and have a good time," she said before heading off to greet more guests.

Sean looked across the room at his father, who had his arm around Matt's shoulder and his other hand around a scotch on the rocks, his standard drink. His father and brother stood amongst a few of Robert's most important business associates.

"This boy's going places," Sean could hear Robert announce loudly to the group.

"Heard you're planning on playin' ball for Ole Miss, son," said Billy Langton, a grizzled man's man who had made his fortune on catfish farms in the Delta.

"Hopefully, sir," Matt responded dutifully.

"Ah, he's a shoo-in, this boy of mine," Robert said, beaming.

Sean turned around and headed back inside, wondering once again why he bothered to come here.

Out of the corner of his eye, Matt could see Alison walking up to talk to Javier. He better not get any ideas about Alison, Matt thought. She was off limits. Everyone knew that Alison was his, and that was the way it was always going to be.

"You ever think about getting' into the catfish business, Robert?" Matt heard some business guy say to his father.

Figuring now might be a good time to exit discreetly, Matt started to head off in that direction, but he felt his father's grip on him tighten. He had not finished showing off yet. Sometimes, Matt hated football and everything about it. People expected what felt like everything from him.

***

"You're the new guy at school," Alison said, smiling, as she walked up to Javier, who sat on a bench outside the backyard gazebo. It was trimmed with neatly-tended flower gardens of fall orange and reds.

Adriana, standing next to her brother, rolled her eyes.

"I'm going to see if I can find Mom," Adriana said before walking off.

"Something I said?" Alison said.

"Nah. Excuse my rude sister. She has a permanent attitude these days," Javier replied. He held out his hand. "I'm Javier."

"Alison."

"I've seen you at school, too. Surprised to see you here."

"Matt's my boyfriend," she said. She glanced in Matt's direction and saw him looking over at her and Javier with suspicion in his eyes. She'd seen that look many times. Whenever she came within ten feet of another guy, Matt looked at her like she had betrayed him. It felt suffocating.

"My dad works for his dad," Javier said. "He's a construction foreman."

An awkward silence fell between the two.

"So, how do you like it here so far?" Alison asked.

"It's...uh...different," Javier replied.

Alison grinned. "Compared to? Where'd you move from?"

"Los Angeles."

"Wow!" Alison said, genuinely impressed. "Hollywood! I've always wanted to go there to visit. You know, see Hollywood Boulevard and the ocean."

"It's not as exciting as it may sound like. But, it is very different here," Javier said. His eyes scanned the room, he noticed that yet again, besides his family, there were no other Latinos at this party.

"What's it like there?" Alison asked.

She found herself standing just a little bit closer to him, drawn to him. She could smell his scent. Was it a cologne or just him? Whatever it was, it sent tingles through her body.

"It's big, busy, goes on for ever, lots of traffic. Lots of other Latinos," he said.

"Well, we have a lot more Mexicans here since the storm," Alison said. In her mind, she cursed herself. That sounded so stupid, she thought.

Javier chuckled. She didn't know if it was because he was offended or because he thought she had actually said something funny.

"I mean...you know...uh," Alison stammered.

"Yeah, it's okay. I've heard that a lot from people since I've been here. But to me, after living in a place where over half the population is Latino, this isn't much of a Latin community," he said. "And not all Latinos are Mexican. There are a lot of other countries in Central and South America, ya know?"

"I'm...uh...sorry," Alison said, blushing.

"Really, it's okay," Javier said. "I didn't mean to make you feel bad. I guess I just get asked a lot of the same questions since I've been here – questions I'm not used to getting back home."

"You should hang out with Matt and me and our friends sometime. There's not much to do around here...not like L.A., I bet. But we can find ourselves some fun sometime. There's the beach, water skiing in the summer, alcohol is easy to get if you know the right people," she said, winking.

Javier wondered if she was flirting.

"I bet," he said, hiding his amusement. .

And out of the corner of his eye, Javier could see Matt's hateful stare.

"Carmen, I don't believe you've met Beverly yet," Kate said, introducing the two women as they stood on opposite sides of the spinach dip.

"Carmen. Nice to meet you," Carmen said, setting down her plate of fruit and cheese to shake Beverly's hand. "My family just moved here."

Beverly nodded her head and smiled as if this point had already been figured out.

"Her husband, Enrique, works as a site supervisor for Robert's new development," Kate said.

"Ah, yes, the Pine Lanes development down Highway 90. That's going to be a huge new development. Beautiful new homes I hear," Beverly replied.

"And Beverly's husband, Don, is Robert's lawyer."

"Well, Robert and Kate throw quite a few shindigs throughout the year," Beverly said. She grabbed another plate and began piling on the finger foods.

"Are they always this lavish?" Carmen said. She watched the cater-waiters in their crisp white uniforms expertly making their way through the crowd with trays of food and drink.

Kate smiled, pleased at her guest's compliments.

"Always," Beverly said.

"Unfortunately, we have had to downgrade this year," Kate said. "It's just not the same, not like at our former house before the storm."

A look of sadness swept over Kate's face, and Beverly looked down at her plate of food.

"This is a new home?" Carmen asked.

Kate put on her best polite smile.

"Yes, we lost our previous home in the storm. Over twenty feet of water swept it all away."

"I'm so sorry to hear that," Carmen said. "I can't imagine. Where did your family evacuate to during the storm?"

An uncomfortable moment of silence transpired. Carmen looked over from Beverly to Kate and back again. Had she asked something off limits?

"Actually, my family was here during the storm," Kate said.

"Oh, my goodness. I can't imagine," Carmen said.

She looked over at Beverly, who stared down at her plate of food, and wondered what must have happened.

"Robert had insisted on staying… at the time," Kate said, her words beginning to trail as if she were in her own thoughts and far away from this party. "He kept saying he had lived through Camille and Betsy, and he wasn't about to let this storm drive him away from his home."

"Men," Beverly muttered under her breath.

"You know how they are," Kate said.

Carmen nodded but wasn't sure she really followed.

"By the time we realized just how bad it might be, it was too late to go anywhere," Kate said.

Carmen thought she saw the beginnings of tears in Kate's eyes, but the woman quickly regained her composure.

"The important thing is my family survived it all, and we had enough money to rebuild. I insisted to Robert that we would not build so close to the water again. I just couldn't...take that chance."

A few more moments of awkward silence passed while Beverly's eyes followed the cater waiters and their trays of food.

"Where did your family move from, Carmen?" Beverly asked to break the silence.

"Los Angeles."

"Hollywood!" Beverly exclaimed. "Now that must be fun. I can't imagine moving from there to a boring, small town Mississippi."

"Well, it has its charms here," Carmen said, trying to stay positive.

"I always wanted to go to Hollywood," Kate said to herself more than the other women. "I always wanted to see some movie stars, Sunset Boulevard, the Santa Monica Pier, the Walk of Fame."

"It's one of those things that if you live there you rarely go to those places."

"So, you've never seen any movie stars?"

"Well," Carmen said, "I did see Chuck Norris once at a Bed, Bath & Beyond."

Beverly's eyes grew wide.

"I can't imagine anything so exciting," Beverly giggled. "Anyone else?"

"Uh," Carmen said, thinking back. "Bob Barker was at the Hollywood Christmas Parade one year."

Beverly looked almost beside herself as she clutched her pearl necklace.

"Mr. Price Is Right himself?"

"Yes, him," Carmen said, laughing.

"If you two will excuse me, I'm going to check on things in the kitchen," Kate said. She also wondered where Matt had disappeared to.

Matt went into the upstairs bathroom and locked the door behind him. He could still hear the crowd downstairs laughing and talking. The band his mother had hired had just started playing some New Orleans jazz.

He looked down at his shaking hands and took a deep breath. He wanted to punch the wall like he had done upstairs in the attic a few times. He couldn't do it here though. His mother would notice the slightest change in the wall. Any indention or chipped paint would give him away.

He felt anger rise through his entire body. Everyone down there either paraded him around to show off, like his father, or they openly disrespected him, like Alison talking to that Mexican kid. Nobody down there really cared about him, about who he was inside. His father had planned his whole future for him, all of his expectations, all of his dreams. His mother spent all of her time trying to make sure they appeared to be a perfect family. His queer brother popped in only when it pleased him, leaving Matt to shoulder all of his parents' hopes for the future.

Matt knew he had to pull himself together – fast. They would be looking for him soon, all of those people with their expectations, their plans for him.

He turned on the faucet and began to splash water on his face. The cold liquid made him gasp and he began to remember.

"Matt! Hang on!" he heard the rescue worker yell through his bedroom window.

"Hurry!" Matt yelled back, panicking at the sight of the rising water outside.

"Get back from the window!" he heard another voice call out.

The sound of shattering glass pierced his room, sending a cascade of water over the windowsill. The room quickly began to fill with water – dirty, brown,

*shockingly cold. The boat right outside his second story window made a loud
thumping sound as it crashed into the side of the house, the unforgiving wind
still demonstrating its power.*

An arm covered in a slick yellow sleeve reached through the window.

"Quick grab my hand!" the first voice called out.

"Matt! Honey, are you in there!" Matt heard his mother's voice
call out as she knocked on the bathroom door.

He groaned under his breath.

"Yeah, what is it?" he asked annoyed.

"Are you all right? Are you coming back down? We're about
to cut the cake."

Matt looked at his flushed reflection in the mirror.

"I'll be down in a minute, okay?" he called back.

There was silence for a second, and then he finally heard his
mother's footsteps walk away from the door.

He gripped the bathroom vanity to steady his shaking. Then
he did what he always did when he had to snap himself out of this,
and when the memories, the demands, the looks, the expectations
became too much. He reached into his back pocket, pulled out his
wallet, opened it, and took out a sleeved razorblade.

He unbuttoned his jeans, pulled them down to his ankles, followed by his underwear. He parted the usual section of pubic hair
in his crotch that concealed his secret from everyone, and he began
to cut into his flesh with the razorblade. The piercing pain of the
blade shocked his body's system and forced him to forget everything else from the past and the present.

He watched the blood begin to pool out from the cut for a
moment before pressing a tissue against the wound to help it clot.
The pain and the blood reminded him that he was still alive.

Sean had had enough of the small talk with people he didn't know
and decided to escape upstairs to the guest room and kill some
time surfing the internet. The strangeness of being in his parents'
new house still struck him. His old room had washed out to the
Gulf of Mexico along with so much else in town.

He thought maybe he should give Caleb a call just to say hi. He then realized that that sounded stupid. He barely knew him. What would Caleb make of that?

As Sean came around the corner into the upstairs hallway, Matt walked out of the bathroom.

"Mom was looking for you," Sean said.

"I'm headed downstairs. Damn!" Matt said, passing him by.

"Matt?" Sean called out.

Matt turned around, annoyed.

"Yeah?"

"You know I don't come back home often. You can at least act civil. You don't have to be such an asshole. You've ignored me the whole time," Sean said.

"Whatever," Matt said. "I don't even know what to say to you, dude."

He turned around and headed down the stairs, leaving Sean standing in the hallway. He felt a wave of sadness regarding his brother, but then decided that Matt was right. The two had always been so different. What could there be to talk about anyway?

"Thanks again for coming," Kate called out to the last guests leaving, before shutting the front door. Finally, she took a deep breath and felt all of the pressure that came from hosting such an elaborate gathering slip away. Robert had tried to tell her he just wanted a quiet dinner out, but Kate had reminded him these parties were important for business.

"Last guest leave?" she heard Sean say.

She turned around to find him standing at the bottom of the staircase.

"There you are. Where have you been most of the evening?"

"Just upstairs relaxing," he answered.

"Upstairs?" Kate said. She hated that he did that every time he came home to visit. "There's still some food in the kitchen. Hungry?"

"Nah, I'm going to head up and crash. My flight leaves at ten tomorrow," Sean said, starting to head back up the stairs.

"Sean!" Kate called out.

He stopped and turned back around. "Yeah?"

"Love you. Thanks for coming," Kate said, smiling a sad smile.

"Love you, too, mom," he said before bounding up the stairs.

Lying down in bed in the unfamiliar guest bedroom, Sean tossed and turned most of the night. His eyes kept glancing at the alarm clock. The minutes felt like they dragged by throughout the night.

In this new house, he felt even more disconnected from his family and his childhood, as though he had just stopped by at some distant relative's house for a family reunion populated with many people he'd never even met.

He tried to concentrate on the relief he would feel when his plane took off the next morning. Each time the plane climbed another thousand feet, the pressure that weighed down on his chest would grow lighter and lighter, and once he'd landed in San Francisco he'd feel like he could breathe again.

Chapter 5

Sean felt so nervous he couldn't even eat a bite of the red velvet cake he had ordered to go along with the half-caf/half decaf coffee he had ordered. It took him a couple of weeks, but thanks in part to A.J.'s insistence, he had worked up the nerve to ask Caleb out for a cup of coffee. Nothing too big, nothing to read too much into, but it was still something. God knows it was a huge step for Sean, who had always waited for someone else to make the first move.

"You're not getting any younger," A.J. had told him one day at work.

"Yeah, well, thanks for the update," Sean had told him.

"You've got to learn to start making some moves where men are concerned. Remember, everyone wants to be the one who's asked to dance."

Finally, one day while volunteering, not long after getting back from Mississippi, he had finally asked Caleb out for coffee under the pretense of thanking him for all of his help.

Now, sitting across from Caleb at a coffeehouse in the Castro, he couldn't seem to think of a damn thing to say. He wondered if his nervousness was apparent.

"So, how was Mississippi?" Caleb asked.

"It was…uh…Mississippi," Sean said. That sounded so stupid, he thought to himself.

"All of your family is there?"

"Pretty much, yeah. I went for my dad's birthday party. It was okay. I just get a little bored usually when I'm there."

"No meeting up with old boyfriends?" Caleb asked.

Sean chuckled, and he just knew he had probably blushed.

"No old boyfriends there," he replied.

"Well, I find that surprising," Caleb said.

"Why's that?"

Caleb cocked an eyebrow. "Because you're so cute."

Sean could feel himself blush.

"Well, uh, thanks," he said. "I think you're pretty cute, too. The whole time I was back home I kept trying to work up the nerve to ask you out when I got back."

"Really?" Caleb said, sounding genuinely surprised.

"Jeez, I sounded like such a dork, didn't I?" Sean said.

Caleb reached over across the table and laid his hand on top of Sean's. He said, "Not at all."

"This is the reality, Matt," Mr. Conner, the guidance counselor at Matt's school, said to him one afternoon after class. "You know you can't stay on the team if your GPA falls below a two. And you know if want to get into a university to play football, you're going to have to graduate from high school first."

Matt had received a summons last period to report to the counselor's office. He knew it would be bad.

"It's algebra. I just don't…get it," Matt said.

"Looking at your past grades I don't see where algebra would be such a challenge. Are you sure you're really applying yourself?"

"Yes, damnit," Matt said, a little too loudly.

Mr. Conner looked a little startled.

"Sorry," Matt said. "It's just frustrating. I have to stay on the team. You don't understand. If I get kicked off the team this year, I won't be able to play in college. My dad…"

"What about your dad?"

"If I don't play, he's going to be really pissed at me," Matt said.

Mr. Conner noticed Matt's foot tapping and hand wringing. It had grown worse in their past few meetings. After twenty years of experience, Conner could sense a kid who was really in trouble. Something had been off with Matt for a while. He had also known Matt's father since they were in high school. He knew how much Robert pushed his kids.

"I would think he'll be even more pissed with you if you don't graduate from high school," Conner said.

"Yeah, I'm not sure about that," Matt said. His gaze drifted toward the window.

"Look, Matt, why don't you let me talk to your parents about getting a tutor for algebra?"

Panic swept over Matt's face.

"Please, no, Mr. Conner. Don't tell my parents yet. Please. I'll get it together. I promise. I'm not going to fail algebra."

Mr. Conner sighed.

"At least let me talk to your teacher about getting you a peer tutor. Okay? I'll give you a little bit more time, but if your grades don't improve I'm going to have to talk to Coach and your parents. Understand?"

Matt nodded. He then glanced out the window, onto the school's front lawn, and saw Alison talking to Javier. Again.

"How's it going?" Alison asked. She wore her cheerleading uniform for practice, and she couldn't help but notice the once-over Javier had given her when she walked up to him.

Yeah, Alison had a boyfriend. Matt had been her first and only real boyfriend. But she had to admit to herself that it was senior year now, and she began to wonder what she might be missing out on by just dating Matt. Sure, he was captain of the football team. Hot. Jockish. Most of the other girls at school would probably kill to date Matt and have the social standing that came with that. So why did she find herself looking a lot at other guys? Especially

Javier? And they were going to college soon anyway, right? How would things possibly continue with Matt then anyway? Every time she thought about bringing it up to Matt, though, she got scared. She had seen him when he got angry, and it was not a fun place to be. Shit, it was downright scary. Not that he'd ever physically hurt her, but still.

"I was headed off to the library to do some research for a paper," Javier said.

"Cool," Alison said for lack of knowing what else to say. This guy's dark intense eyes were downright dreamy. He also had a worldliness about him that Alison, being someone who wanted to see so much more of the world than she had in her hometown, found attractive. Javier just wasn't like the other boys at school. He seemed so much more like a man and someone whose thoughts could go further back than this Friday's football game or who had the next keg party.

"Are you...uh...off to practice?" Javier asked.

"Yeah, I guess I better go," Alison said. "See you around."

"See ya," Javier said.

Javier watched Alison walk away. Damn, she was hot. Shame she had a boyfriend.

"Yo, dude!" Javier heard someone say behind him.

Javier turned around to find Matt headed his way and looking pissed off.

"Yeah?" Javier asked. He stood up a little straighter, stiffer, giving the "tough" look he had learned to perfect hanging with his friends on Alvarado Street in L.A, a sometimes sketchy part of town where you could buy yourself a new set of identification papers, various drugs, or a prostitute. His parents would have locked him in his room if they had known he was hanging out there. Although he had never taken any drugs or done anything illegal, at least not very illegal, he got a certain thrill being in danger's alleyway.

Matt bounded towards him and pushed him against the outside brick wall.

Javier bounced back, and pushed Matt away from him.

"Dude, what the fuck?" Javier yelled.

Matt stood before him, breathing hard, his face bright red. The guy looked like he could explode at any second.

"I'm only goin' to say this once. You need to remember who the fuck your dad works for, and you need to stay away from my girlfriend!"

"Chill out, man. I never touched your girl."

"Yeah, and make sure it stays that way, wetback," Matt said, before storming off to his SUV in the school parking lot.

It took every bit of restraint Javier had not to take Matt and his small town country ass down. He had no idea the things Javier had seen and things he had dealt with on the streets in his barrio. The things he knew his parents wanted to keep their kids away from. But what Matt said about his dad kept playing over in his mind. Why the hell did his dad have to work for this nutcase's family? He knew his dad would crap his pants if Javier got into a fight with his boss's son. Even though it bugged the hell out of him, he knew he should probably just stay away from Alison. Dealing with her jerk boyfriend just wasn't worth it. *Was it?*

"You could help me fix dinner. Your father will be home soon," Carmen said to Adriana, who was watching the TV placed on the breakfast table in the kitchen.

"Why can't he help, too? Why is it always me?" Adriana said, glaring across the table at Javier, in the middle of algebra homework.

Carmen sighed and then abruptly said, "I'm going to the store to pick up some things. If you could check on the chicken in the oven, that'd be great."

After their mother let, Javier said, "So, are you going to check the chicken?"

"The chicken is fine, okay?" Adriana said, turning the channel to MTV.

Javier groaned, got up, walked over to the oven and checked on the chicken.

"I guess it's okay," he said.

Adriana remained silent. She took a bottle of nail polish out of her purse and began to do her nails.

Javier slammed his algebra book shut.

"What's your problem?" Adriana asked.

Javier sat back down and took a deep breath.

"Look, Adriana, I know you're not happy to be here. I'm not either. But do you have to be such a bitch?"

"A bitch?"

"Mom's trying, you know. So is Dad. You don't have to make things even harder."

"You don't understand. You're a guy!" Adriana exclaimed.

"What does that mean? That's crazy!" Javier exclaimed. "You think I don't miss home? My friends? The basketball team? Everything I used to know. You don't know shit, Adriana."

Javier saw tears begin to come out of his sister's eyes. Usually, he saw her crying as nothing more than attention seeking. But this time he actually felt sympathy for her. Maybe some sort of brotherly love surfaced, or perhaps deep down he wished he could shed some tears, too. His machismo would never let him, though.

"Just, damn, Adriana. Can't you be nicer," he said, looking away.

"Ever since I was a little girl I used to dream about my *quincenera*," Adriana said, referring to a fifteen years old Mexican girl's celebratory party honoring her entering womanhood. "Mama, Tia Theresa, Nana, and I have been talking about it since I was a little girl...what kind of dress I'd get, the food, the flowers. No one here even knows what a *quincenera* is!"

"That's why you're all pissy though? About a party?"

"You don't get it, Javier. You just don't get it," Adriana said, starting to get up.

"Look, I'm sorry. Okay? It's just that this move is hard on all of us."

At that moment, Ever came running through the kitchen with a new neighborhood friend around his age.

"Outside! Charge!" Ever yelled, while he and the other boy ran out of the house.

"Except maybe him," Javier said.

Adriana wiped her eyes with the back of her sleeve.

"I'm sorry about your *quincenera*," Javier said. "Just because we're here doesn't mean you can't have it, ya know?"

"It wouldn't be the same," Adriana said quietly.

"Maybe," he replied. "Just try and be easier on Mom. She's trying hard to make this work. I don't think she wants to really be here, either."

Adriana looked out the kitchen window at Ever playing with his new friend in the yard.

"Why'd we have to come here? Christ. I hope it ends up being worth it to *Papi*."

A burning smell started to drift through the kitchen.

"Shit!" Javier exclaimed. "The chicken!"

"Did you see 'em, man? Standing outside the hardware store? All those Mexicans. Everyday there's like more of them. What about our men? What about their jobs?" Beau said, shaking his head. He and Matt hung out on Beau's carport while they installed a new stereo in Beau's Toyota truck.

"Yeah, there's a ton of 'em working for my dad. Cheap workers, I guess. But that one, that kid from school, I don't like him," Matt said.

"The one Alison checked out at school?"

Beau dropped a screwdriver on the floorboard of the truck.

"Man, you don't know what the fuck you're talking about!" Matt said, his face turning bright red with anger.

"Hey, chill man. I'm sure it's nothing," Beau said, backing off. "I just don't know why all the Mexicans are piling in here. I mean don't they have their own country?"

"Their own country?" a gruff but female voice said behind them.

The two boys turned around to see Beau's grandmother, Tillie, walking out onto the carport.

At eighty years old, Tillie carried a strong dignified grace with her. She always, always, got fully dressed and made up every day just in case someone should happen to stop by. Her still thick silver hair hung in short braids around her face. A retired teacher, she had lived and taught through the height of school segregation.

"Grandma!" Beau said, caught off guard. His grandmother always had the ability to make him shape up behavior-wise just by her presence. And as she'd been living with his family since the storm, Beau had got away with a lot less.

"Hi, Mrs. Wilton," Matt said.

Both boys got out of the truck and simultaneously smoothed down their shirts and pants.

"I must say I'm disappointed to hear such words coming out of your mouths. *Their country.*"

Tillie made her way over to pick up her watering can.

"Well, grandma," Beau began, "You got to admit things seem to be changing around here...and fast."

Tillie paused for a moment as if she were considering this information.

"Not too long ago you two boys wouldn't be standing together here...being friends. It wouldn't have been allowed."

"But that's different," Beau protested.

"Different how? That's always what people say. It was different when it was us. You think about that," Tillie said, heading out to the back to water her plants. "The only sure thing in this life, boys, is change."

Kate seldom went into Matt's room. Just the clutter and messiness that came with being a teenage boy was enough to send shivers down her spine. How anyone could live in the middle of such chaos she'd never understand. So she usually was content with just letting him keep his door shut. But her sister, Carol, from Tupelo, was going visit later in the day. Carol had not seen the house since it had been completed, and she'd want to see each and every room. If it weren't for the fact that Carol's house practically shone from every angle because of its cleanliness, Kate wouldn't be bothered. But she and her sister had always shared a little bit of sibling competition.

So Kate decided to take the plunge while Matt was gone and at least straighten up her son's room a tad. She could at least pick the clothes up off the floor, throw the comforter over the bed, and make sure no obscene pictures of half-naked women were tacked on the walls.

Kate slowly opened the door as if a monster may be lurking inside, waiting for a trespasser. The room looked worse than she had even dared to think.

"Good lord," she said, surveying the mess.

She began to pick up the clothes from the floor, including the dirty gym socks that could be smelled from at least five feet away. She had to hurry before Matt came home and go ballistic at finding her in his space.

She picked up perfectly clean t-shirts she had just washed and handed to him in the hallway that morning.

"Can't even be bothered..." she began to say as she opened up one of the dresser drawers to put away the t-shirts, only to find the drawers were just as unorganized. Something metal in the back of the drawer caught her eye.

She pulled the drawer out and discovered three small straight razors.

"What the hell?" she said, shaking her head.

Why did he have these stashed in this drawer?

"Mom!" she heard Matt call out, and she quickly stuffed the t-shirts inside the drawer and closed it.

Matt walked in the room. A look of panic and then anger swept over his face.

"What are you doing in here?" he demanded.

Kate studied the look on her son's face. She'd always been able to sense when Sean or Matt were keeping something from her. He looked beyond annoyed. He looked scared. She immediately knew he didn't want her to see something in this room...and it was big. Drugs?

"Your Aunt Carol is on her way, and you know she'll want to see the whole house. I just had to straighten up a little in here. I don't want her to think you live like a savage in here."

"Damnit! Can't I get any privacy around here? Can't you show me just a little respect?" Matt yelled.

She noticed his hands were shaking.

"Son, calm down," she said softly.

"Just leave me alone in here, okay? That's all I ask. Please?"

Now he showed a look of desperation mixed with fear.

"All right. Just trying to tidy up," Kate said, walking out.

Matt slammed the door behind her.

She knew she'd have to go back in...and soon.

"Well, I must say, you've done a remarkable job getting this place together so quickly," Carol said to her as the two of them strolled in the backyard, admiring the flowers.

Sometimes Kate couldn't be sure if what her sister said was meant as praise or a backhanded compliment.

"I've tried my best," she said.

Carol nodded, as if more could have been done, somehow, under her guidance.

"And how's Robert's new business venture?" she said, pausing to take a sip of the fresh lemonade Kate had given her.

"Coming along. A lot of work though. It's turning into his biggest development yet.

Carol nodded and smiled.

"Well, that's wonderful," she said, smoothing down the skirt on her crisp navy blue dress. "And the children?"

"Matt's senior year. I can't believe it. Seems just like yesterday he was my little baby," Kate replied. The nagging thoughts of finding those razor blades plagued her.

"Time goes by quicker than we'd like," Carol replied. "And how's Sean, you know, in San Francisco?"

She said the name of the city in sort of a half-whisper as if Sean's living there had been a big secret.

"He's good. I wish you could have been here for the party. He was here."

"That must have been lovely to have both of your boys in your new home…for once."

"Yes, it was," Kate said.

"Is this a magnolia tree you've planted over here?" Carol said, walking off.

Kate's mind went back to the huge magnolia that had graced their backyard before, and the sweet scent of their blooms, back when everything seemed so much simpler…and straightforward.

Chapter 6

"Hey, Javier," Alison said.

Javier looked up from his table at the library to find Alison standing before him looking cuter than ever, if that was possible.

"Hey, Alison," he said. He felt suddenly self-conscious about the old baseball t-shirt he wore. "I'm here doing some research for that paper in Ms. Ladd's class, and I...just needed to get out of the house."

"Yeah, me, too," Alison said.

They both fell silent. Javier glanced down at his book. Alison readjusted her backpack on her shoulder.

"Could Ms. Ladd's class be any more boring?" Javier asked.

"Oh, I know. I'd rather go to the dentist," Alison said.

She wanted to look at his eyes, so dark, the color of a midnight sky.

"Wanna sit down?" Javier asked.

He wondered if it sounded too hopeful. He had to play it cool. What about that jealous boyfriend of hers? That was Matt's problem to deal with, not his. He was only talking to her anyway.

"Sure," Alison said.

She pulled out a chair and placed her bag on the table.

"We could do some research together," she offered.

"Yeah. Sounds good," Javier answered.

He noticed Alison didn't just give him that elusive butterflies in the gut feeling: he could have sworn there was a swarm of bees in his stomach.

"Sometimes I just have to get out of the house to get anything done," she said, opening her bag and taking out her books.

"Yeah, my little brother is usually running around the house making noise or wanting me to go outside and play soccer with him."

"I wish I had a brother or sister," Alison said. "Someone else that could understand my family dysfunction."

"You look like you have the perfect family, though. Your family seems like they have a lot, you're popular, a cheerleader, dating the quarterback, and," he paused for a second before taking the real plunger, "you're pretty."

His forwardness made her even more excited, and more daring than usual herself, "What about you? You come from the big city, you've seen so much, and you're handsome."

"I don't know about all that," Javier said, feeling suddenly shy.

"I do. All the girls at school do."

"Nah," he replied, trying to act nonchalant. Did all of the girls at school really think that? But most importantly, Alison felt the way he did?

"I guess we better get some work done, huh?" Alison said, opening her notebook.

"Yeah, I guess so," Javier said. He paused, and then added, "Thanks for the compliment."

For Sean and Caleb, coffee had turned into dinner at a Thai restaurant. Dinner had turned into dessert at a bakery in the Italian neighborhood of North Beach. Dessert had turned into hot tea at Sean's apartment in SoMa. Luckily, Sean's roommate, a straight artist from New York, had gone back East for a showing. So Sean had the whole apartment, all 500 square feet of it, to himself.

Hot tea had, of course, turned out to be a pretense for an intense make-out session on Sean's futon with the purple mattress. Sean had expected things to go much further, but Caleb had stopped suddenly.

"I think we should slow down a little," he had said, before adding, "For tonight."

Sean smiled.

A guy who wanted to wait? How romantic! Or maybe he had three testicles, or maybe he had a boyfriend. A raging case and colony of crabs?

The guy, the date, everything had just gone too well. Hadn't it? Or had he just gotten way too cynical for a guy in his early twenties? Sean let his mind run wild as Caleb gently laid his head against his chest, wrapping his hand around Sean's arm.

Sean had first arrived in San Francisco to attend college at Cal State, and he thought he'd just landed in the middle of a gay Disneyland. While growing up in his small Mississippi town, he had only caught a few short glimpses of gay life in parts of the French Quarter in New Orleans. Here, in San Francisco, and not just in the Castro, gay people appeared to be everywhere living openly. Sean would never forget the surge of power he had felt on one of his first days in San Francisco, when he took the MUNI to do some shopping at Union Square. When he emerged from the subway underground, he saw a male couple, not much older than him, walking down Market Street holding hands. Nonchalantly. As if it were nothing, and no one around them seemed to notice, much less care.

He had mostly kept to himself as a teenager, flying under the radar while his parents appeared to gush attention on his younger brother. During his senior year, he announced he wanted to attend college in California. His father surprisingly agreed.

"It'll do him good to get out on his own," Robert had said.

His mother tried to talk him into going to some place closer, but after Sean got offered a full academic scholarship, she relented.

During college, he rarely went home except for short Christmas visits. Following graduation, he found a room to rent in SoMa and made the Bay Area his permanent home.

Caleb shifted his weight on top of Sean's body and sighed. Sean noticed Caleb's breathing turned into a soft, rhythmic pattern. He'd fallen asleep.

Sean always had had a problem actually sleeping in the same bed with another man. He didn't know if it was a trust issue or just plain intimacy.

Caleb obviously didn't have the same problem. This both excited Sean and scared the hell out of him.

Around Alison's family's dinner table not much was ever said. Usually she, her mother and her father ate their food while the evening news droned on in the background. This evening proved to be no different. Her mother had prepared one of her father's favorite meals, and one of Alison's least: meatloaf, mashed potatoes, and green peas.

Alison picked at her food. She couldn't get her mind off Javier and how entranced she felt every time she saw him. She wanted to know everything about him. What he dreamed about for his future. About his life in California. How he felt being in a place so different. How he got so handsome.

"Alison, honey, are you not hungry?" Beverly asked.

"Not really," Alison answered.

"It's important that you eat," Beverly remarked.

Alison took a bite of mashed potatoes to quiet her mother. Her mother knew she hated meatloaf, but for some odd reason every time Beverly made it and Alison protested, Beverly would say with a look of surprise, "But I thought you liked meatloaf!"

"Don, honey, more meatloaf?" Beverly asked.

Don's eyes briefly strayed from the television screen in the background.

"Sure," he said.

Alison sighed. She glanced down at the family's dog, a poodle named Tee Tee, who sat next to Alison's chair in the hopes that some stray morsels may hit the floor. If her mother got up and her father looked distracted, Alison would give Tee Tee a healthy portion of her meatloaf.

Alison then noticed what looked like a cigarette burn on the bottom of her mother's khaki pants. But it couldn't be! Her mother never smoked and complained about smokers all the time. It had to be something else.

She looked back up at her mother, and Alison realized she must have had a strange look on her face.

"Anything wrong, dear?" Beverly asked.

Alison shook her head no.

Beverly looked over at Alison's plate and her untouched food. "Honey, I thought you liked meatloaf."

Tee Tee barked loudly, and jumped up, putting her freshly painted pink toenails on Alison's thigh.

"Down, Tee Tee!" Beverly commanded. "You have your own food."

After her sister left, Kate immediately poured herself a glass of wine. Robert had stayed out of the women's way, retreating into his study. Only now did he emerge, probably because he heard his sister-in-law's car pull out of the driveway.

"Carol left already?" he asked, walking into the kitchen.

Kate smiled.

"As if you're upset by that."

"Hey, I didn't say anything," Robert said, holding up his hands.

"Um...hmmm." Kate took a sip of wine. "Do you know if Matt is home?"

"Think he left to meet a friend," Robert said, pouring his own glass.

"I think something's wrong with Matt," Kate said, sitting her glass down.

"Wrong? The kid's got everything," Robert said, shrugging his shoulder.

Kate grunted. Robert had never been known to have much of a softy side. In his mind, if you had money in the bank and your physical health, what the hell could be wrong?

"Robert, I'm being serious. I went into his room earlier today to clean up before Carol got here, and he…well…he went ballistic on me. I just have a bad feeling there was something in that room he didn't want me to find."

"Yeah, like maybe some girlie mags. What kid would want his mother to find that?

"You've been buying him porno?" Kate demanded.

"No, I have not been buying him porn," Robert replied. He sat down on one of the kitchen barstools. He didn't know why his wife had to make such a big case out of anything with one of their kids. "He's a teenager. He's just going to be protective of his space, trying to assert his independence."

Kate shook her head. "No, I don't think that's it."

"He shouldn't have gone off on you though. I'll talk to him about that as soon as he gets back."

Kate groaned. "That's not what I'm worried the most about. I think…"

She started to tell Robert about the razor blades in a weird location, but Robert's cell phone rang.

"This is Enrique. Gotta take it," Robert said, answering the phone and walking out of the kitchen.

Kate wrapped her arms around herself. She didn't care what her husband said. Her gut told her something with her son was off.

"Man, don't you find it kinda depressing to hang out here?" Beau asked.

He and Matt, drinking beers, sat on the remains of the front steps that once led to Matt's house, the house that had existed before the storm. Surrounding them was lot after empty lot where once grand houses stood next to the Gulf of Mexico. All of the houses had been swept away by storm surges over twenty feet high.

The only traces that someone had lived there were the concrete slabs on the ground, the occasional front steps to nowhere, and the remainders of piers that led out over the Gulf.

"I like coming back here," Matt said. "I wish we still lived here."

His eyes scanned the area. Nothing had really changed since the storm, except maybe some clean up. All traces of the childhood home he knew, such as the old tree house in the now dead oak tree, and the back porch where he used to watch football with his dad, had been wiped away in mere minutes.

Beau placed his empty beer can on the ground and crushed it with his foot.

"It's just, you know, with all the shit that happened here to you and stuff..."

"Dude," Matt said, popping open another beer. "It's not like I could forget all of that if I wanted to."

"You still ain't said much about it."

"Don't want to talk about it," Matt said. "It's on my mind enough as it is."

"Yeah, I bet."

"There is something I haven't told you though. Or my parents. Or anyone on the team."

Beau cocked his head. Matt had never been one to say much about his life anyway.

"Like what?" Beau asked.

"I'm probably going to be kicked off the team," Matt said quietly. "And it'll be before homecoming."

"What the fuck?" Beau said. He stood up. "You can't leave the team. Man, we need you. Why the hell would you be kicked off? That doesn't make any sense!"

"I'm failing a class. My counselor said there's no way around it."

"Well, get a fucking tutor, dude!" Beau exclaimed.

Matt jumped off the step and immediately got in Beau's face.

"What? You think I haven't thought of that? You think I want to fucking leave the team? Huh, Beau?"

Beau stepped back and looked at his friend. He'd never seen this look of rage come over his friend, even in the closest of football games.

"Dude, I'm just saying..." Beau began.

Matt threw his beer on the empty concrete slab behind them.

"You don't know shit!" Matt spat, before turning to walk away.

"Yo, man, wait up!" Beau called after him, but something told him to let Matt cool off.

"Hey, what are you doing up?" Beverly asked Alison when she walked into the living room past midnight that night. An infomercial for a food dehydrator played on the TV in the background.

"Couldn't sleep. Thought I'd get some milk," Alison replied. "What are you doing up?"

Alison sat next to her mother on the couch. Their pink pajamas practically matched. In fact, sitting in this position, in these clothes, many people would have sworn that Alison could be the younger version of her mother.

"Couldn't sleep either," Beverly said. "Been happening a lot to me lately."

"Are you okay?" Alison asked, concerned.

Beverly placed an arm around her daughter.

"I'm just fine! Just a little insomnia. Got all wrapped up in channel surfing."

They watched the infomercial for a few moments before Alison said, "Can I ask you a question?"

"Sure."

"I've been thinking about something," Alison confessed.

"I knew something weighed on you right now."

"You like Matt, right?" Alison asked.

Beverly nodded.

"Sure. He's a good kid from a good family," Beverly answered. She then cocked an eyebrow. "Why? You're not thinking of getting married are you? Are you pregnant?"

"No, Mom!" Alison said, exasperated.

Beverly sighed. "Okay. Then why did you ask what I think about Matt?"

"It's just," Alison said, shrugging her shoulders. "He's the only guy I've ever really dated, and…"

"You have eyes for someone else?" Beverly asked.

"I don't know," Alison said, hesitating.

"Hmmm…I think you do know," Beverly said. She squeezed her daughter's shoulder. "So, who is he?"

"Javier," Alison answered.

"Ah…." Beverly said. "The new boy. The one from Los Angeles. I met his mother. She was very nice. And when I saw him…he definitely was a very handsome young man. Those dark eyes!"

"He's gorgeous," Alison cooed.

"You've got it bad!" Beverly said, laughing.

"And sweet. He actually listens to me when I talk, unlike Matt. Matt never asks me what I think or feel about anything," Alison said, pausing. "But I've been dating Matt all through high school."

"Look, sweetie," Beverly said, taking her daughter's hand. "High school is just high school. It's only a few years of your life. At the time it may seem like the whole world, but it's really only a road stop for you. It's natural for you to want to date some other guys. See who else is out there. Find out what's right for you."

"So, you think it's okay if I end up dating him," Alison said.

"Of course! You're young. You have so many years ahead of you. If you like Javier, then you should spend some time getting to know him."

"It's going to be hard to tell Matt though," Alison said softly. "I don't want to hurt him. I really don't."

"I know, sweetie. But sometimes getting a broken heart is part of life. We learn from it. It may be good for Matt to date some other girls, too," Beverly said. She sighed. "Oh, sweetie, life goes by so fast. I know it may sound corny, but it feels like only yesterday I was your age, my whole life ahead of me. Promise me you won't be scared to explore things in life and go after your dreams. We only get one shot at this thing called life you know. Promise me."

Alison could detect a sense of urgency in her mother's voice.

"I promise," she replied softly, before adding, "Mom, are you okay?"

Beverly smiled, but it was a pained smile.

"Of course, I am! Now how about we tackle some of that homemade vanilla ice cream I have in the freezer?"

Chapter 7

Sean couldn't believe he had slept in so late when he looked at his clock. He and Caleb had had dinner together again. That made three dates in three days. A record for Sean!

He reached over to the other side of his bed and remembered that Caleb had left earlier that morning, saying he had to get ready for work. He gave Sean the sweetest, softest kiss on his forehead. After that, Sean went back to sleep. To sleep! He had actually slept peacefully and soundly.

He stretched and wiped the sleep from his eyes. He stumbled out of the bed, a big grin on his face, thinking about Caleb's arms holding him, his lips kissing his neck, the heat of Caleb's body radiating warmth throughout him.

He walked into the bathroom, switched on the light, and opened the fly of his boxers to pee. That's when he noticed it sitting on the counter next to the sink. Neatly folded and placed there, as if its owner would be back soon, was a pair of socks.

And Sean freaked.

"It's a pair of socks!" T.J. told Sean over lunch at a sandwich shop in Nob Hill.

Sean put down his tuna on rye and moaned.

"But it's what they represented!" he protested.

"What?" T.J. said, mouth half-full of pastrami. "The socks represent something?"

"Well, yeah!" Sean said. He ran his fingers through his newly highlighted hair that Caleb had complimented just the night before. "The socks spoke volumes!"

T.J. rolled his eyes.

"So, you're telling me that socks speak now. I know you go a while without doing laundry, but…"

"Oh," Sean said. "You're just making fun of me."

"No, dear," A.J. said. "It's just that I think you're making a huge lasagna out of small side of pasta."

"Don't you get it? The socks were placed there as if their owner would be returning- soon! It means he has expectations. Expectations! What if I let him down? What if…"

"What if he hurts you one day? Is that what you were going to say?"

Sean looked out the window at the passer-bys rushing between lunch and work. Everyone went by in a hurry. No one appeared to notice much around them, such as the way the sun shone brightly in a very un-San Francisco way, the older Asian lady who sat on the corner waiting for the bus, and the young enthusiastic group of children being led by an exasperated teacher on a field trip.

"Sean?" A.J. said. "Is it that you're scared you may have met an amazing guy who you click with? That you might put yourself out there and maybe even get hurt?"

"I don't know. Maybe," Sean replied.

A.J. picked up his pastrami sandwich for another bite, but first he said, "Well, then don't fuck it up!"

A.J. and Sean looked at each other. Sean smiled.

"I'm going to really try not to," he said.

"Don't try. Do," A.J. replied.

One second Javier was telling Brent he'd see him in chemistry class, the next he was thrown against the wall by the lockers. His head began to ache and the thud from the sound of the impact rang in his ears. Then he felt Matt's hand around his throat as he tried to lift him from the floor.

Various voices began to call out.

"Hell, yeah!"

"Fight! Fight!"

"Kick his ass, dude!" Beau yelled.

Javier slammed his knee into Matt's crotch and Matt released his grip.

Finding his balance again, Matt bounced back and stepped up, filling Javier's field of vision. Javier heard only the chants in the background.

"Fight! Fight! Fight!"

Matt's face loomed inches from Javier's, to the point where he could smell the catsup from lunch on Matt's breath.

"What the fuck's wrong with you, man? What's your problem?" Javier demanded.

Matt looked at him, glaring.

"I told you to stay away from my girlfriend," he growled.

Good and pissed now, Javier had no clue what Matt had seen or heard to get him so worked up. But obviously the guy felt threatened.

Javier pushed Matt back and smiled slyly.

"Don't know what you're talking about, man," he said.

Matt started to charge towards him again, but at that moment the football coach and the shop teacher pulled them in opposite directions.

In the principal's office, Matt and Javier sat across from one another, avoiding eye contact, but still working on some old fashioned male posturing.

The principal, Mr. Graham, who prided himself on having a so far violence-free year, suspended both of them for a day and demanded that their parents be called immediately to pick them up, with further threats of a week of in-school suspension.

Robert and Enrique came close to colliding when they both entered the office. The two stopped, looked at each other, turned and looked at both of their sons sitting there. Both boys looked angry and disshelvd.

"What the hell?" Robert demanded.

"Javi!" Enrique exclaimed.

"Good. You're here to get your sons," Mr. Graham said as he walked out of his office. "I trust that both of you will take care of this situation so it doesn't happen again."

Matt and Javier both averted the scornful eyes of their fathers.

Robert and Enrique looked across the room at each other, boss and worker, two fathers, and realized their sons had been fighting each other.

"What were you thinking, *mijo*?" Enrique demanded when they got into the car.

Javier stared out the window.

"I'm speaking to you, Javier!"

"You didn't even ask me who started it," Javier said finally, still avoiding eye contact.

"I don't care who started it. That's irrelevant!" Enrique said.

He reached into his pocket and pulled out a piece of gum that he began to chew furiously.

"Are you going to start the car?" Javier asked, his voice tainted with a hint of spite.

"Don't you dare use that tone of voice with me! That is not how your mother and I raised you," Enrique said. He reached over and grabbed his son's chin, forcing Javier to face him. "He's my boss's son! What were you thinking?"

"I told you I didn't start it!"

"You want me to lose my job? Is that what you want?" Enrique asked.

He began to soften when he saw that his son's eyes were beginning to tear up. He hadn't seen Javier cry since he had been four years old and his cat died.

Javier jerked his head out of his father's grip and turned it so Enrique wouldn't see the tears he fought back.

"None of us wanted to come here. You're the one that made us," Javier spat. "You didn't even take us into consideration."

"What are you talking about? Your mother and your brother and sister are the reason that we are here, that I moved us across the country, and that I'm working so hard."

"We were fine back in California! Don't make this sound like you did it for us just because you wanted to prove something again to Mom's parents," Javier said. He felt emboldened. He had never dared to speak to his father with such candor, and his father appeared to be perplexed at how to handle it.

"I moved us here so we could have a better life, more money to help you kids go to college," Enrique said, his hands shaking slightly. *He had, hadn't he?*

"Can we just go home? Please?" Javier asked.

"This is not over," Enrique promised.

Robert swerved the family's Ford Explorer angrily along the same curve he always warned Matt to be careful of. The only words he had uttered to his son were, "In the truck. Now!"

"Are you going to say anything?" Matt asked finally.

"I'm too mad at you to say anything," Robert said, slamming his hand on the steering wheel. He glanced over at his son. What the hell was wrong with him? It's not that the kid got into a fight that struck him, but that he did it with the son of the man who was to be his right hand man. Matt had screwed with his business.

"That kid made a move on Alison," Matt said as if he and Javier weren't the same age.

"Alison!" Robert exclaimed. "Son, you're about to graduate from high school. You'll be going on to college. It's time you realized that this is probably the end of you and Alison."

"What?" Matt said, sounding genuinely hurt.

"High school is almost over," Robert said, pulling up to the family garage. "It's time you started acting like a man."

"A man?"

"Unless you're more like that brother of yours than I thought," Robert said, his voice filled with a level of disgust that even struck him as extreme.

"I'm nothing like Sean, and I never will be!"

"Well, then," Robert said, taking his key out of the ignition. "Then I expect you not to embarrass me at this stage of your life. Got it?"

Robert hopped out of the SUV leaving his son sitting inside, seething.

Javier sat on the couch while Carmen sat next to him, checking for cuts and bruises as only a mother would. Enrique paced back and forth in front of the television on which a weather forecaster spoke of unseasonably cold temperatures.

"I can't believe you got into a fight," Carmen said, finally satisfied that her son had not been severely injured. "How could this have happened?"

Adriana walked into the living room.

"What happened?" she asked.

Carmen sighed.

"Your brother got into a fight," she said.

"With my boss's son!" Enrique added.

"Was this because of that girl?" Adriana said. "I heard rumors around school."

"Be quiet, Adriana!" Javier commanded.

"What girl?" Enrique said, finally stopping the pacing.

"Uh…I gotta go," Adriana said. She tried to head back to her room, but Enrique blocked her way.

"What girl?" he asked even louder.

"Please, Enrique, we don't need the neighbors to hear all of our business," Carmen snapped.

Enrique turned to Javier.

"What girl?" he repeated.

"Matt thinks I'm going after his girlfriend," Javier finally admitted.

"You're what?" Enrique said. His face turned bright red.

"It's all in his stupid head!" Javier said.

"It better be. And I want you to stay away from that girl, too. We don't need any trouble," Enrique ordered.

Javier jumped up from the couch.

"That's not fair!" he protested.

"What's not fair is you not thinking of your family first, *mijo*," Enrique replied.

"I'm out of here," Javier said, heading towards the door.

"Don't you leave when I'm talking to…" Enrique said. The sound of the front door slamming stopped him. He looked down at Carmen, who sat on the sofa shaking her head, and then at Adriana, who seemed disturbed by the scene.

"Let him cool off for a moment, Enrique," Carmen suggested gently.

Adriana quickly headed back to her room.

"All this over some girl?" Enrique said.

Carmen got up from the couch and began to walk past him.

"Isn't that what your parents called me? Some girl?"

Matt stared at himself in his bedroom mirror. He had to put himself in check. He couldn't keep losing it, but when Beau mentioned seeing that Javier guy with Alison, his Alison, he freaked. No matter what his dad said, the end of high school did not determine the end of their relationship.

He reached into his drawer and dug around for the blade. Right now it would be the only thing that could shock his mind off what was going on, how everything seemed to be falling apart on him, quickly and steadily.

A knock on his door broke him out of his trance.

"What is it?" Matt yelled out.

"Matt. It's Alison. Your mom said I could come up. I need to talk."

"Just a sec," Matt called back.

He quickly shut the drawer and checked himself out in his mirror. He still looked like he'd been in a fight, so he quickly put on a new t-shirt, slicked back his hair with some gel, and wiped his face with a tissue.

"Matt?"

He opened the door to find Alison standing there, her eyes red from crying.

"Hey," Matt said. "You okay?"

He leaned in for a kiss, but Alison moved back.

"Can I come in?" she asked. Her eyes darted from side to side down the hallway. "I'd like to talk in private."

"Yeah, sure," Matt said, moving aside.

Alison walked in, and Matt shut the door behind her. Usually, Alison would have sat down on his bed, which ultimately would have led to a make-out session. This time, however, she sat on the chair at his computer desk, putting obvious distance between them.

"Hey, what's wrong?" Matt asked, kneeling down next to her.

"Everyone at school is talking about it. How could you pick a fight with Javier, Matt? What the hell were you thinking?" she demanded. Her face flushed red with anger.

"Beau told me…" Matt began.

"Christ, Beau told you what?"

He reached for her hand, but she quickly pulled it away.

"Beau said he saw that guy making moves on you at the library," Matt said. "What did you expect me to do? Just sit back and let him mess with my girl?"

Alison jumped up. She began pacing back and forth across the room.

Matt slowly stood up. He didn't understand her. Wouldn't she want him to fight for her? To warn any other guys to back off?

"Baby, I did what I needed to do," Matt reasoned.

"What you needed to do? Are you crazy?" Alison said. She stopped pacing and took a good look at Matt. After all their time dating, maybe her mother had been right. If Matt didn't give her what she needed, why did she put up with it? And now he had picked a fight with Javier for no good reason.

"First off," Alison scolded. "Javier and I were only doing some homework together at the library. We just ran into each other. You remember homework, Matt? It's one of those things we have to take really seriously since we're seniors now. We can't afford to goof around."

"I don't want to talk about school. That's not what this is about!" Matt said, grabbing one of her arms.

She shook him off and said "Don't touch me!"

"What's wrong with you?" Matt asked. He felt his heart race and his right hand shook. He wanted to just hit something right then. Hit something hard.

"What's wrong with me? What's wrong with you?" Alison said, pointing at him. "Nothing happened between Javier and me. Nothing. Maybe you could have asked me before you ran off and decided to start hitting him."

Matt tried to steady his breathing, regain his focus. No one ever thought he did anything right. He didn't know what people wanted him to do to make them happy.

"All right, maybe I should've talked to you first, but I was upset," Matt tried to reason.

Alison shook her head and folded her arms.

"This just isn't working, Matt. It hasn't been for a while. I think we both know it, too," she said.

Matt, shocked, stepped back.

"What do you mean?

"It's just things between us…we've never dated anyone else, Matt. And I think we should do that. We're seniors now. We'll be going off to college soon."

"That doesn't mean anything," Matt said. He took her arm again, out of desperation, and pulled her to him. "We love each other. That's all that matters."

Alison slowly peeled herself away. She'd begun to cry now and she wiped her eyes on the sleeve of her high school sweatshirt with the pirate logo.

She gazed up and her eyes met his.

"I don't want to hurt you, Matt," Alison said, her voice cracking. "But I don't think I'm in love with you."

Matt stumbled back a step, the words striking him like a direct blow to his heart.

"You don't love me?" he said.

Immediately, Alison wished that she had somehow said what she needed to say very differently.

"I...just think...we need to go our separate ways and see how it goes."

"You're breaking up with me, huh?" Matt said, his voice sounding eerily void of emotion.

Alison nodded.

"I'm sorry," was all she could think to say.

Matt's gazed fixed across the room, away from Alison.

"I think you need to leave now," he told her.

"Matt..."

"Leave!" he commanded.

Without saying anything else, Alison walked out of the room, shutting the door behind her.

Chapter 8

The second morning bell had just rung, and Javier rushed to grab his chemistry book out of his locker. His whole family ran late that morning just because Adriana got a hot curling brush tangled up in her hair. Her screams had been so frantic, Javier thought she sounded like someone who had just been stabbed. Instead, he ran to the bathroom to find her with the curling brush hanging from the side of head.

"I just tried to straighten it," she cried.

Javier busted out laughing. He simply couldn't help it.

"It's not funny, Javier!" Adriana screamed. "Mom! Help!"

The last thing Javier needed was to get into any more trouble at school. Even the slightest little thing would tick off his dad big time.

He grabbed the chemistry book out of the locker and as soon as he turned around he found Alison standing there.

"Hey, do you have a minute?" she asked.

He wondered why she wasn't in class.

"Look, Alison, uh..."

"I'm sorry about what Matt did," she said. "Are you okay?"

She reached out and gently touched his arm.

He noticed how she smelled faintly of roses and everything he fantasized about when he thought about Alison.

"Look, I'm sorry, but I gotta get to class. The last thing I need is anything out of line after yesterday," Javier said, regretting it as the words rolled out of his mouth. He thought of his dad, Enrique's job, and his father's warnings to stay away from Alison.

"Oh, okay," Alison said softly. "Later then?"

"Uh, I'll see you. Okay?" he said, turning away and walking off before he could change his mind.

Kate stood in the doorway to Matt's room. Instead of heading into her and Robert's office, she had told Matt she had a headache and would be staying home that morning. She didn't want to arouse his suspicion.

Matt had long gone to school, and she headed up the stairs with the idea of going through every inch of her son's room for a clue to his odd behavior. Yet, now that the time and the opportunity presented itself, she hesitated.

As she gazed at Matt's unmade bed, the empty cereal bowl next to the computer, the sports trophies carefully arranged on a wooden shelf, Kate felt guilty. What did this say about her as a mother that she would stoop to spying on her son?

It's true that Matt hadn't been the same since the storm. But who would be living through what he had?

"I told you we should have evacuated, Robert!" Kate had cried, as the rescue workers took them to safety. "Why did you insist we stay? Why in God's name did I listen to you?"

For weeks after the storm, Matt had barely said a word.

Robert immediately threw himself into his work and rebuilding their home, and Kate followed. They both thought that putting all of their energy into bringing order back to their life should be number one. Had they failed Matt, though, and themselves, by not talking about or dealing with what had actually happened, what had been taken away, and what had almost been lost?

She almost turned around and left the room chalking up all of her recent feelings to old-fashioned paranoia and being overprotective. She thought of the razorblade in the drawer and just how out of place it seemed.

Just to be safe she walked across the room, opened the drawer, and carefully moved items around, so as not to stir up suspicion, to see if the blades were still there. She breathed a sigh of relief when she saw they were gone. But then she realized that just because they had disappeared didn't mean the blades weren't somewhere else, and what was Matt doing with them in the first place?

As much as she tried to push her worries to the back of her mind, they still plagued her.

"Coach, please! There's gotta be something you can do. Right?" Matt pleaded.

In the counselor's office, Matt paced back and forth. Mr. Conner, the counselor, sat at his desk. Coach Thompson, all legs in short gym shorts and beer belly, stood with his back leaning against the wall next to a poster that reminded seniors when to apply for college financial aid.

Coach shook his head. "Jesus, Matt! How could you let it get this far?"

"Did you get the extra tutoring I suggested?" Mr. Conner asked.

"Right! How was I gonna fit that in between my regular classes and practice? This just isn't fair," Matt said, balling his hands up into fists by his side.

"You do what you need to do to take of business, Matt," Coach said, furiously chewing a piece of gum. "You know how much the team depends on you. But there ain't...I mean isn't...anything I can do. You know how strict the school is about this, especially after those school board meetings last year about us bein' too easy on the athletes."

Mr. Conner watched as Matt's pacing continued.

"You mind if I have a second alone with Matt, Coach?" he asked.

Coach raised his hands.

"Have 'em. Ain't nothing I can do with him now."

Coach walked out of the tiny office and shut the door behind him.

"Matt, why don't you have a seat?" Mr. Conner asked, gesturing towards the visitor chair.

"Don't feel like sitting," Matt said.

"Humor me," Mr. Conner said sternly.

Hesitantly, Matt sat down.

"Did your parents get the letter from the counseling office regarding your being taken off the team?" Mr. Conner asked.

"Yes," Matt lied. He had beaten his mother to the mailbox and tore up the letter.

"How did they take it?"

"How do you think? They weren't happy."

He had no idea how he'd tell his parents this, especially his father. They'd both be so disappointed in him. Coach was right. How had he let this happen? How had he let everything happen?

"Well, I know how important the team is to your dad."

"Yeah, tell me about it," Matt said.

"Matt, do you think a lot about the storm? About what happened? To you?"

"What do you mean?" Matt asked, shifting uncomfortably in his chair.

"Well, Matt, you went through a pretty traumatic event. You had to be rescued because your family didn't evacuate."

"They didn't know it would be so bad!" Matt said defensively.

"No one did, Matt," Mr. Conner said, quietly, soothingly. "My point, though, is that sometimes when we don't emotionally deal with traumatic events in our lives our minds have a way letting those buried feelings impact other parts of our lives. I can tell a big difference in how you've been dealing with and reacting to things since the storm. Have you talked to a therapist about any of these feelings?"

"I don't need a head shrinker," Matt said, furiously.

"It's not like that," Mr Conner said. He folded his hands and set them on his desk. He noticed Matt shaking his left foot, darting his eyes all over the room but not making contact. He knew he would have to contact his parents and express his concerns. But he also knew Matt's father, the traditionalist. Sending Matt to a therapist would be a hard sell, but maybe if he could get through to the mother. "I want you to promise me something, Matt."

"What?" he asked. Why were people always making demands on him?

"If you ever do feel like you need to talk to someone…about anything…I want you to let me know, okay?" Mr. Conner said. He reached into his desk and pulled out a card and wrote a number down on it. "I don't normally do this, but I want you to have my cell phone number. I want you to call me at anytime you feel like you might need to talk."

Mr. Conner held out the card, and Matt just stared at it. Deep down part of him wanted to talk, talk so badly about how he'd felt since the storm. He wanted to talk about the cutting. He wanted to unburden his mind with all of the worries that constantly swirled around in his head like an ocean undertow pulling him down lower and lower each passing second. But if his parents ever found out, it would be worse than dying. He'd already be such a disappointment to them by being kicked off the team.

"I won't need it," Matt said at last, glancing at the card.

"Will you take it anyway? Put it in your wallet? For me?"

Matt hesitated, but then reached over and took the card out of Mr. Conner's hand.

"I should go to class now," he said quietly.

Instead of class, though, he headed to the upstairs restroom, the one where not many students went, and locked himself in a stall. He took out his wallet, and looked at the card Mr. Conner had given him. He knew the guy had just been trying to help him, but what could he really do? What did he understand?

He took the razorblade, sleeved by two one dollar bills, out of his wallet, unbuckled his pants, and began to cut – watching as drops of his life fell into the toilet water below.

***

Enrique sat at the dining room table paying bills and balancing the checkbook. Carmen walked up behind him and wrapped her arms around his shoulders.

"Dinner will be done soon," she said, bending down and placing a kiss on his cheek.

"Look at this bank balance," Enrique said, pointing to the checkbook. I told you this move will be good. Just one year of being here and we'll finally get ahead."

"Last time I checked we'd been ahead for awhile," Carmen said.

She moved some of the paperwork and sat on the table.

"But now we'll be far ahead," Enrique said. "More money for Javi going to college next year."

"Speaking of Javier," Carmen said. She reached down and held her husband's hand. "He really does like that Alison girl, and she seems really sweet."

"And she's also dating the boss's son. She has to be off limits for him."

"Remember my parents saying the same about you?" she said. "And vice versa?"

"This is different," Enrique said, closing the checkbook.

"Is it? Really?"

"Yes, he just met this girl. She's not worth him screwing up everything he's worked for, that we've worked for."

Carmen walked to the other side of the table, pulled out a chair, and sat across from her husband.

"What about what Javi wants? He's almost grown now."

"So, you think I'm out of line?"

"I think you're concerned for your son and your family, as you should be," Carmen began. "But you know the more we try and keep him from seeing that girl...well, you know."

"I know, I know," Enrique moaned.

***

"Brent said you were working here part-time," Alison said, walking up to one of the construction sites.

Javier dropped the discarded two-by-four he had just picked up and wiped the sweat from his brow.

"You came looking for me?" he asked, surprised but deep down, happy.

Alison dropped her purse next to the front door of the skeleton of someone's future dream home.

"Yep," she said. She walked around on the concrete floor of the barely-framed living room. "You ever think about who will be living here one day?"

"Nah. Not really, to be honest. Too many houses being built at once to think."

"So, how do you stay on top of school and work?" Alison asked. She noticed the straining of his biceps under his tight UCLA t-shirt.

"I need to save for college," Javier answered.

Awkwardly, Javier tried to get back to work, feeling Alison's eyes watching his every move.

"Why'd you brush me off this morning?" Alison said, getting to the true point of her visit.

"Yeah, I, um," Javier started to say. "You know after the fight and stuff at school, my dad...you know Matt's dad is his boss."

"So because of that we can't hang out?" Alison asked with a mixture of annoyance and hurt. "I thought we had some spark."

"What about Matt?"

"I think it's time I moved on. Things between us haven't been...good in a while. So, that's not in the way," she said, moving closer to him.

Alison reached out and touched his arm. Javier could have sworn he felt his heart skip a beat.

"Your dad's job is the reason we can't see each other?" she asked.

He shook his head.

"I want to get to know you, too," he said.

"So?" she said, smiling.

"So what?" he said, smiling back.

"Then take me to the homecoming dance."

Her boldness made her even more attractive in his eyes.

"Homecoming, huh?" he said, stepping further into her space. He thought of his father and his warnings, but decided he had to start being his own man. "It's a date then."

He leaned in and kissed her, passionately and aggressively, just as he'd been wanting to do for so long.

Sean had decided to take T.J.'s advice and try not to freak out about the sock situation. Instead, he decided to take matters into his own hands and invited Caleb over for dinner. Sean had never been much of a cook, neither had his mother. In fact, growing up they ate more food from caterers and delivery people than off their own stove. But what he did have a knack for was putting together a great salad – organic greens, fresh seasonal vegetables, some braised tofu, and a tangy honey mustard dressing he'd found the recipe for while leafing through a Reader's Digest in the dentist's office.

With the candles on the table lit and two glasses of Merlot waiting, Sean served Caleb as close as he came to home cooking on the new dinner plates he'd bought at Crate & Barrel, just for this occasion. He'd really made an effort at romance this time, for a first.

"Wow! It looks beautiful," Caleb said. "Very healthy. Much better than the corn chips I had for lunch."

"Thank you. It's sort of my only…um…dish," Sean admitted. "Most of my food comes straight from the freezer."

He waited anxiously for Caleb to take his first bite, and when he did and smiled with his approval, Sean let out a sigh of relief. All this domestic stuff was new territory for him.

"Very good," Caleb said. "Great dressing."

"Old family recipe," Sean said slyly.

"Ah, I meant to ask you," Caleb began. "Did I leave some clothes here the other night? I was looking for a particular pair of socks the other day."

"Yeah," Sean said. "They're back in my bedroom."

"Sorry about that. I thought I had gotten everything before I left."

"No problem," Sean said.

Deep down, beyond the place where he kept things on the surface, safe and secure, Sean knew a little disappointment resided in his heart now. He never would have admitted it to anyone, perhaps not even to himself, but part of him wanted to read something into that pair of socks.

"More wine?" Sean offered.

Caleb got up from the table and walked around to him.

"I think I'd rather have a kiss," Caleb said, bending down and planting a passionate one on Sean, the kind of kiss that makes your heart rate increase, the heat move through your body.

Matt leaned back against one of the decaying oak trees along Beach Boulevard. Traffic remained light on this side of the highway since parts of a connecting bridge over St. Louis Bay had collapsed during the storm, isolating the two sides of the coastline from each other, and the only sounds Matt heard were seagulls squawking above.

He watched the waves hit the beach as the sun began to set. He knew time would be running out soon. His parents would find out about him being kicked off the team, his chance at playing at college level over. Everyone would hear that Alison had dumped him. He heard the ticking on the alarm clock of his life grower louder with each passing second.

He looked out over the water and saw the remains of a pier where his grandfather used to take him fishing. Those afternoons fishing under the bright sun, drinking Barq's root beers and eating Moon Pies, were some of Matt's best memories of being a little boy. The pier, like his grandfather, no longer existed in his life.

Things that meant the most to him continued to be taken away in what felt like seconds, over and over again.

He thought about Mr. Conner's card in his wallet and wondered if he should have talked about what he had been feeling, what he had been doing. But then he wondered what Mr. Conner could possibly do to help him. In what way could talking about how fucked-up his life had become help?

He reached under and pulled his wallet out of his back pocket, and took out the guidance counselor's card.

"I know. I just worry. I can't help it. I worry about us, Matt, and Sean," Kate said, once again having nagging thoughts about Matt's personality changes, the razor blades, the maternal knot in her stomach that kept insisting all was not right.

"Everyone is just fine," Robert insisted.

The kitchen door slammed shut, and Matt came stomping in the house.

"Hey, son. How are you?" Robert said.

"Okay," Matt muttered under his breath.

"You want some...?" Kate started to say, but before she could offer her son any of the pound cake she had made earlier that evening he had already stormed out of the room, and she could hear his quick footsteps bounding up the stairs.

"He's in a hurry," Robert said, taking some more Mylanta.

"He's always in a hurry these days it seems," Kate said. She walked over to her purse and took out her cell phone to charge it as she did every night. Ever since the storm she'd been borderline obsessed that her phone stayed charged. She didn't know why, since the cell phone towers had gone down anyway.

She noticed she'd missed a call.

"I have a message. I didn't even hear the phone ring. Too busy worrying about you," she said to Robert.

"I'm fine, fine," he replied. "Check it. Make sure it's nothing about the site."

But before Kate could dial her voicemail and retrieve the message that had been left by Matt's high school counselor, Mr. Conner, to call her regarding Matt; before she could have her worst thoughts and suspicions confirmed, gunfire rang from upstairs.

She froze and looked at Robert, whose face had gone pale.

Chapter 9

Including all of Robert and Kate's business associates, practically the whole local high school, and relatives, the church service had been standing room only. After all, Matt's family had always been well-known in town, and he had been the school's star athlete. The kid that people thought had everything had done the unthinkable. He had taken his own life.

Only a fraction of the people at the service showed up at the burial, to give those closest to him more privacy in which to grieve. Also, many people just didn't know what to say to Kate and Robert.

The day of Matt's burial it didn't exactly rain, but instead it turned misty as the mourners stood around the coffin on that chilly October Saturday afternoon. The crisp moist air kept the flowers colorful and in bloom. More than one person had been overheard saying, "I've never seen more beautiful flowers at a funeral."

When a young person dies as the result of an accident or disease the nearby community often rallies around the parents, offering their support and condolences. Suicide, however, can spark a different reaction. There can be a certain level of awkwardness in the air mixed in with the grief. People sometimes just don't know what to say when it comes to suicide. The cause of the death becomes a taboo subject; the big, loud, pink elephant in the room that no one is mentioning. This was especially true in Matt's case.

Standing next to her son's coffin, Kate amazingly had enough self-awareness to know that she was not truly present. She had not allowed herself to be in the moment from the second she heard the gunfire, ran up the stairs, and discovered her baby, his face covered in blood, on the floor. She couldn't allow herself to feel and still get through everything that had to be done.

Robert immediately fell apart, stayed at the office, and spent almost every waking moment drinking and sobbing. Kate had to work hard to get him to leave his flask at home for the service and burial. No matter how badly she wanted to throw herself over her son's grave and scream and cry, she held back.

She noticed the quick glances and the whispers everywhere she had gone the past few days, from the flower shop to the department store to buy a new dress for the funeral. She'd imagine what people were saying to each other.

"How could she let that happen?"

"Did no one notice that something was wrong?"

"The boy had everything. Why would he shoot himself?"

While going about the business and frenzy a death in the family brings, Kate kept replaying the same things in her mind over and over.

She remembered the nurse handing her Matt right after the delivery. Even though she knew people would've said it couldn't be possible, she knew that the baby had looked up at her and smiled as if to say, "Finally. I'm here."

She remembered the numbness she felt listening to the voice-mail from Matt's guidance counselor to please give him a call. He had some concerns about Matt.

The words of the investigator, Detective Williams, an older man with a kind face and deep blue eyes, "There's a set of cut scars on his body that are consistent with someone being a 'cutter,'" he told her.

Kate had shaken her head, not understanding. Robert, too lost, couldn't even stand to hear what the detective and the reports had to say. Kate marveled at how men, who are supposed to be so strong, were usually the first to completely break down.

"What do you mean by cutter?" she had asked the detective, sitting across from him on her front porch, clutching the glass of tea she had insisted on pouring for both of them.

"It's a phenomenon we are seeing more and more of in teens. It seems to have gained in popularity, for lack of a better word, with boys. They do it to try and block out some other pain."

"What do they do to themselves exactly?" she asked quietly, not knowing if she wanted the answer.

The detective sighed and set his glass of iced tea down on the small wicker table next to his chair. He folded his hands in his lap and his eyes met Kate's.

"The victims cut themselves intentionally. They usually do it in a place that they can conceal. Some cut their arms and then wear long sleeves to mask the scars. Some, like Matt, do it in the groin area."

Kate gasped.

"I'm so sorry to have to tell you this," Detective Williams had said.

"Me too, Detective," Kate had replied. "Me too."

She remembered the razorblade, out of place, in Matt's drawer. Her initial concern - and later convincing herself that she had been trying to make something big out of nothing - haunted her like a shadow that followed her everywhere.

The day after Matt's suicide, Robert had to leave the house for a night when the cleaning crew came to wipe away her baby's blood. She had stayed and even supervised the cleaners.

Sean had immediately flown home, and he'd been a great help. Somehow he knew to do things she didn't even have to mention: picking out a suit for Matt, making an appointment with her hairdresser for an evening when no other clients would be around, and picking up Robert at his office. Both of them knew he shouldn't be driving with his drinking. He even cleared out the kitchen and organized all of the food that came pouring through their front door. As if she could possibly feel like eating.

And now between her remaining son and husband, standing by her Matt's closed coffin, she wondered how much everyone would hate her if they knew she had had the power to save her son. She knew something was off, despite what Robert said. She had seen the razorblade. She had missed the call from the guidance counselor. She had let her son die, and she knew she had made it even worse by keeping all of these secrets to herself . How could she live with herself after this? But she had to hold it together for her son's funeral. She owed her child that much.

Alison had been unsure at first if she wanted to go to the burial site after the service. She came very close to getting sick right there in the church looking at Matt's closed coffin, knowing he was in there, and thinking about what he had done to himself. As morbid as it was, she couldn't stop herself from wondering what he looked like lying in his coffin and what the shot to his head had done to his face. She knew it had to be bad for the coffin to remain closed. Matt had always been so handsome. She couldn't imagine.

Her mother, and of course Javier, had been the only ones that she had talked to about breaking up with Matt. Was all this on her? She had known Matt was upset, but she never dreamed he would do this. How insensitive must she have been?

When most people saw Matt she knew what they saw – a rich kid, popular, star athlete, cocky. But during their years of dating she had seen another side of him. Often when it had been just the two of them, maybe in his car parked by the beach or under the bleachers after a game, he'd reveal a different side of himself. When there was no crowd to show off for, Beau wasn't around to goad him on or he didn't feel like he had to save macho face, Matt could actually be tender with her. He'd hold her close to him and tell her some of his deepest secrets, like the fact that he wasn't nearly as confident as he acted and he didn't know how to deal with his brother being gay. He'd tell her how much pressure he felt from his family to excel at everything and that he still had night-mares since the storm.

But then everyone had problems, right? She would have never thought that Matt would, or could, do this to himself. Had he really loved her that much?

She stood next to her mother in the back of the crowd at the burial. She couldn't bear to look Matt's parents in the eyes. If she had been the cause of Matt killing himself, how could she possibly ask for their forgiveness? How could she ever love anyone else, including Javier, if she knew the dangers love possessed?

Just a week ago, Sean had been shopping at a home décor store in the Castro feeling a rush of domestic urges since dating Caleb. And now here he was back in Mississippi and serving as a pallbearer at his own teenage brother's funeral. It all had been so surreal. The night Matt killed himself Sean had had an uneasy feeling he couldn't explain. Something kept nagging at him in the pit of his stomach. When his mother called the next morning with the news, he went into shock but a part of him had been expecting some-thing horrible to happen.

Now standing outside at the burial site, wearing shades and a suit that had become just a little too tight over the past couple of years, Sean felt an overwhelming sense of sadness when he realized that he really hadn't known his brother at all. Matt had only been eleven when Sean left home, and before then Sean had spent most of Matt's life trying to navigate the confusion matrix that is the teenage years. On Sean's rare visits home, he avoided his rough and tough little brother not knowing what to say or do with him.

Sean had been old enough to remember Matt as a baby though. He remembered as clearly as if it had been five minutes ago the day his parents brought Matt home from the hospital. Sean ran out of his grandmother's front door to meet his parents as soon as they got out of the car.

Surprisingly, it had been his father who held the baby as they got out of the car. His mother looked beyond exhausted, and it had been one of the few occasions Sean had seen her without make-up.

"I want to see the baby!" Sean had said, jumping up and down.

His father, smelling of aftershave and cigars, knelt down to show him the newborn. Matt, asleep with skin the color of his mother's pink roses, had been swaddled tightly in a bright new blanket.

"This is your new brother, Matt," his father said.

Sean looked at the new baby with wonder and amazement. He couldn't believe how tiny his new brother looked.

"My baby," Sean said in amazement.

And that was how he referred to Matt those first couple of years - my baby.

Sean would sometimes just sit in Matt's nursery and watch him sit or play in his cradle. He loved playing with the new baby and when his mother let him, feed him.

By the time Matt started running around the house on his own, Sean couldn't keep up with him anymore, and that early relationship that had been formed between them slowly grew further and further apart.

Matt barely listened to the words of the priest over the burial site. All he could think about was how much he wished his brother could have remembered those early days and that he could have known how much Sean had loved him before he died.

As Matt's casket was lowered into the ground, the sobs became more audible and the dark skies overhead began to let their first drops of rain free for the day. Suddenly Kate let out a piercing cry, the first one since the terrible event. Sean put his arm around her and held her close to his side.

Kate turned to Robert for his support, but she saw he was already walking back to the car.

Chapter 10

"We will remember Matt and his contributions to the team," Principal Dillon said in the gymnasium during a school assembly the next Monday. He held up Matt's jersey. "Number 42."

Matt's number had been officially retired.

During most student assemblies, it took Principal Dillon at least ten minutes to get all of the high schoolers to quieten down. But today the whole school took on a somber feeling. The school had arranged for extra counselors to be on site to speak with any student who wanted to talk about Matt's suicide.

Beau sat in the front row. The whole school had known the two were best friends, and no one seemed to know what to say to him. In fact, it seemed most people appeared to avoid him for lack of not knowing what to do, or thinking that Beau needed his space.

The only person Beau had had die in his life was his grandfather, when he was three. No one prepares a teenager to deal with the death of his best friend. His grandmother had walked into his room the night Beau had heard the news and just held her grandson. No words were exchanged. None needed to be. Beau began to sob onto his grandmother's shoulder. She was the only person he would have ever allowed himself to be so vulnerable with, and Tillie had known it.

"Let it out, baby," Tillie whispered into her grandson's ear. "It's okay. I'm here."

Now at school, sitting in the auditorium, playing with his watchband, he appeared stony faced as some "expert" got up to speak on teen suicide and how someone should go about getting help.

He knew Matt had been acting strange. Could he have done something?

But more than anything he felt anger at Matt for having done this to all of them. He glanced over and looked at Alison, sitting next to Missy, her eyes reddened from tears. Rumors had it she wouldn't be at school for the whole week because she was so upset. Yet here she was. And Beau then saw Alison make eye contact with Javier, across the gym, and he watched them hold their gaze.

"Robert!" Enrique said, surprised to see his boss show up on the worksite. "We...uh...weren't expecting you today."

Robert surveyed the worksite. Laborers milled about carrying various pieces of lumber while some had a quick sip of coffee from their thermoses to fight off the cold.

"Why not?" Robert asked, slightly slurring.

As Enrique walked closer, he could smell alcohol on Robert's breath.

"We just..." Enrique started to say.

"Robert!" Kate called out.

Enrique turned to find Kate hopping out of her bright red Honda Accord, wearing only a housecoat, her usual finely-coiffed blonde hair haphazardly pulled back into a ponytail.

"I told you I have business to take care of!" Robert yelled back at her.

All of the workers stopped in the middle of what they were doing. The site usually buzzed with so much sound, but now it was so quiet birds in a nearby tree could be heard chirping a morning song.

Kate's face flushed with embarrassment. Her eyes surveyed the crowd and she pulled her housecoat tighter around her waist.

"You need to come home with me, Robert," she pleaded.

Robert, his expression becoming an angry snarl, turned back to Enrique. "You told me the house on the corner would be completed last Friday! The landscaping hasn't even been started."

Kate grabbed her husband's arm.

"Please, Robert! Come with me. We need to go home. You shouldn't have driven!"

Robert shook off her arm and pushed her away when she attempted to hold on to him.

"Everyone in town knows," Robert snapped at Enrique.

Enrique, confused, looked to Kate for some sort of answer, but she looked as bewildered and panicked as he felt on the inside.

"Robert, I'm sorry. I don't know what you're talking about," Enrique said.

He glanced over at the workers, still frozen in their stances.

"Everyone knows your son stole my son's girlfriend from him. This isn't Los Angeles. Word gets around," Robert slurred.

"Robert, I don't know what to say, but I don't think Javier…" Enrique began to say.

Kate grasped her husband's arm again and half-whispered in his ear, "Please, Robert, can we go. You're making a scene."

Suddenly, Robert's internal fire died down, and he looked at his wife with a face of dreary resignation.

"Let's go," Kate said, taking his hand. She turned to Enrique and said, "I'm so sorry."

Enrique shook his head to let her know not to worry about it. But how could he not worry about Robert's ravings? This job put food on his family's table and was supposed to be their future.

"Are you happy now?" Beau asked, cornering Alison in a corner of the school hallway next to the cafeteria right after lunch.

Alison clutched her books tighter to her chest.

"What are you talking about?" she asked, not meeting his eyes.

"All right. That's how it's going to be then?" Beau said. "You do that to my boy, jerk him around. He would've never done what he did if you hadn't broken his heart. But it was all about you, right Alison?"

Alison could feel the tears beginning to sting her eyes.

"Matt did this to himself, Beau," she said, anger rising in her voice. "You don't think I'm upset about this, too? I cared about him.."

"Alison!" Javier called out, quickly making his way down the hall towards her. "You okay?"

Beau, seething, turned around and faced Javier and said before walking off, "You're going to get yours, spic!"

Javier ignored the comment and grasped Alison in his arms.

"You okay?" he repeated.

"No," Alison sobbed. "I'm not okay at all."

"Don't listen to him. He's just a jerk," Javier said. He pulled her closer to him, embracing her.

"He's saying what a lot of other people think, Javier," she whispered.

"Sit down!" Kate commanded Robert. She slammed the kitchen door behind her.

"I'm going to make you a strong cup of coffee."

"Coffee," Robert chuckled, and he slumped down on a bar-stool in the kitchen. "Yeah, that's all I need is a strong cup of coffee, Kate. Then everything will be fine."

Kate dropped the can of coffee on the counter.

"Then what then? Why, Robert? After everything we've been through, did you have to go make a scene in front of all those people? Neither Enrique nor anyone in his family is responsible for Matt dying."

I am, she thought.

"He was!" Robert exclaimed. "Matt was."

"Matt?" Kate said her voice cracking.

"How could he be so weak?" Robert sighed. "I didn't raise him to take the coward's way out."

Kate, shocking even herself, reached her hand over the counter and slapped Robert so hard across the face, the force left a hand-print.

"Don't you ever say that about Matt!" she said. She looked up and saw an astonished Sean standing in the doorway. "Sean!"

"Are you two okay?" he asked hesitantly, standing in the door-way wearing a SFU t-shirt and sweat pants. His hair stood out in all directions, and it struck Kate that he looked like the young teen she remembered. She wished she could go back to that time, somehow keep her family from turning into this. Whatever "this" was.

"No, we're not okay," Robert said, the red imprint from his wife's hand still present on his face.

Kate started shaking and looked down at her hands. She then busied herself with making the coffee as if the exchange had never happened.

"Mom?" Sean said, tentatively approaching her while she sat on the sun porch.

After watching his parent's scuffle he had showered and changed into a crisp blue dress shirt and khakis. He knelt by his mother's side and gently placed a hand on her arm. She turned and looked at him, surprised, apparently just realizing he had returned to the room.

"Hi, sweetie," she said finally. "I'm sorry you saw that scene between me and your father."

"It's okay. Emotions are a little raw right now."

"It's just when he called Matt weak, I snapped," she said.

"Maybe you two should get some counseling to deal with this," Sean said gently. "There are a lot of different emotions that can come about from a...suicide. Anger, resentment, blame..."

"I don't blame, Matt!" Kate exclaimed. "How can I? He was just a boy."

The two remained in silence for a few moments, and Sean stroked his mother's hands. He noticed that they had begun to roughen and wrinkle. The beginning of gray roots in her hair had started to show, something Kate would have never allowed to happen from what Sean remembered. It should have been obvious that of course his mother had grown older, but he had never thought too much about it. During the past few days, Sean realized how disconnected from his family he had become, but then he had no idea how to rectify the situation. He knew how his father felt about him being gay, and his mother often pacified his father, which was why seeing her slap him really threw him.

"I have to head back to California soon, Mom," he said softly. "For work."

A look of sheer terror swept across Kate's face, and she clasped her son's hands tightly.

"Please, Sean, not yet. Stay for a few more days. Please. I ...just...it would make me feel so much better to have you here for a little more. Please, son," she pleaded.

He'd never seen her look so desperate and lost, not even at Matt's funeral.

"Okay," Sean said. "Let me call my boss, and I'll ask for some more time. I'll see what he says."

Sean already knew what T.J. would tell him. He'd say to take as much time as he needed before coming back.

This scared Sean most of all.

Chapter 11

Alison hadn't been able to sleep more than three hours ever since Matt's suicide. She'd spend most of the night tossing and turning in bed thinking about Matt and wondering if she could have done anything to stop him. She also felt a little selfish about feeling so angry at him for killing himself at a time that people would point fingers at her.

"You think he did it because of you?" Betsy, another cheerleader, said to her before practice while throwing her pompoms. "Because if he did, that would be so sad, but in a romantic way."

Every night she'd replay her conversation with Matt in his bedroom when she broke up with him. Should she have stayed with him? Was she betraying his memory still with her feelings for Javier?

One night Alison, out of sheer exhaustion, finally fell into a deep sleep. Matt would not let her rest, though, as he visited her in her dreams.

Alison, lying on the beach in Biloxi, sat up and asked Matt to put sunscreen on her back. The sun, merciless, beat down on their bodies, the heat almost palpable.

"I thought you were breaking up with me. Now you want me to put sunscreen on your back?" Matt asked. He stared straight ahead, sitting on his beach towel, wearing only blue board shorts and shades.

"It's not like you haven't done it before," Alison said.

"It's not like I haven't done a lot of things to you before," Matt replied shyly.

"Maaaatttttt," Alison groaned. "Did you have to go there?"

He cracked a smile but still stared straight ahead.

"Already been there," he said.

"I'll put it on myself," Alison said, squirting some sunscreen in her hand.

"Can I ask something?" Matt said. He stretched his lightly-haired, defined legs out in front of him.

"Sure," Alison said, rubbing the sunscreen on her body.

This is strange, she thought. Isn't Matt dead?

"What is it about this Javier guy? What's he got that I don't?"

"It's not like that, Matt," Alison began. "I didn't mean to hurt you. I honestly think it's just because we're young. I feel like I have so much more of the world I want to see and explore. Javier sort of, you know, stands for that. He's from another place, one that sounds more exciting. He has stories he can tell me that no one else here does. He looks at me in a way no boy, including you, has ever done, like he just wants to melt into me."

Her hand reached over and rested on top of his. She noticed his class ring had become a different color - white instead of blue.

"I truly didn't mean to hurt you, Matt. You were my first love, and you'll always be special to me."

"Really?" he said, reaching up and taking off his shades.

"Yeah, of course."

"You'll always be special to me, too, Alison. I never meant to hurt you either," Matt said.

And then he finally turned around to face her and to her horror Alison noticed the opposite side of his face was covered with blood, with more dripping out of a hole on the side of his head.

"I'll always love you," he said.

Alison sat straight up in bed. She gasped for breath. She felt as if someone's hands had been wrapped around her throat. She wanted to scream but no sound would come out of her mouth.

The only sound was a soft ticking that came from the Mickey Mouse alarm clock, given to her on her eighth birthday.

"Alison!" her father called out as she headed to her car to drive to school.

"Yeah, Dad?" she asked. She felt tired, as if she hadn't had a minute's sleep, despite having been out for at least five hours. The first fall chill wafted through the air, and she suddenly wished she had brought her cheerleading windbreaker.

Her father, wearing his usual suit for work, walked up to her and sat his briefcase down on the driveway. He looked up at the sky as if searching for some answer that would come from above.

"Alison, Alison," he said.

"What's up, Dad?"

"How are you doing with everything? You know, with Matt. You barely come out of your room. Your mother and I are wondering if maybe some counseling would help you."

"I don't want counseling," Alison said adamantly. What if a counselor told her that there had been something she could have done to make a difference? "I can handle this."

Her father awkwardly placed a hand on her shoulder. He had never been good with any sort of affection.

"Only if you're sure," he said. "But if you change your mind I want you to let us know."

"I will. Promise."

This answer seemed to satisfy him and a consoling smile appeared on his face.

"You know I worry about Matt's dad. I hear he's not handling this too well," he said. "I mean, probably no one would. But after all of the years with our business association we've become good friends. And, well, word around town is that Matt may have…now I'm not saying this is your fault, but that your break-up with him might have been some sort of trigger."

"Daddy!" Alison exclaimed. She couldn't believe he was saying this to her.

"I'm just saying this because I know you have a crush on some other boy - a Mexican."

"His name is Javier."

"I just don't think this would be the best time to, you know, for you to get serious with another boy. Let everyone have some time processing what happened to Matt, you know?" He gave her a small hug and picked up his briefcase. "I don't want you to be late for school, so I better let you go," he said.

Alison, her heart heavy, watched her father walk away towards his red SUV.

"Javi, you ready for school?" Carmen asked, popping her head into her son's room.

Javier, wearing a USC sweatshirt, sat on the side of his bed. His back pack, all ready to go, sat next to him. He'd gotten up as always, showered, ran to the kitchen to grab a bowl of cereal, and returned to his room to check and make sure he had everything.

But then it hit him. He felt frozen, unable to leave his room. His feet no longer seemed to be his own as he could not command them to move. Instead it was as if each foot had a five hundred pound block of concrete chained to it. Eventually, he sat on the bed, unsure what to do.

"Mom?" he finally managed to say.

Carmen tentatively entered the room and placed her hand on her son's shoulder.

"Are you okay, *mijo*?" Carmen asked. She felt her son's cheek. It felt clammy. Beads of sweat broke out on Javier's forehead. "Do you feel sick?"

"People blame me, you know?" Javier said, looking up at his mother.

Carmen always knew that her son had a kind soul. The machismo he had sometimes projected when he became a teen was always just a front. She knew it, even if she didn't let on. Growing up, Javier had insisted on burying all of his goldfish after they died, versus just flushing them down the toilet. He never forgot a family member's birthday. She knew he still prayed every night before he went to sleep, and that he sometimes checked in on his little brother at night, tucking him in, putting the blankets that Ever often kicked off the bed in his sleep back in their place.

"Blame you?" she asked.

"For what Matt did to himself. Kids at school. Everyone's talking about it."

"What are they saying?" Carmen asked, sitting next to him.

"That maybe Matt killed himself because Alison broke up with him because she likes me."

"Oh, baby," Carmen said. She wrapped her arm around him. "You and Alison are not responsible for what Matt did to himself. People may never know exactly why he did what he did, but it was definitely not your fault."

"There are people who think differently," Javier said sadly.

"Well, we can't control what anyone else thinks."

"He must have been really sad to do that to himself, though," Javier said, looking down at his lap.

"I know, *mijo*. If that had been you or one of your…" Carmen stopped herself, fearful to even utter the words. "Just know that there's nothing you can't come to me about. Okay?"

Javier nodded his head.

Ever since the detective had told Kate about Matt's cutting himself, she'd become obsessed with finding out everything she could about cutting, as if this might somehow explain to her why her son felt the need to take his life. It also served as a way to punish herself, to give her insight into how her son tortured himself, how she sensed the clues but did nothing.

Every chance she got, Kate Googled articles on teen suicide and cutting. Sometimes late at night, after Robert had drunk himself into an uneasy sleep, she'd sit in front of the computer reading one article after the next.

And this morning, with Robert still passed out in bed, Kate sat in front of the computer and did another internet search, this time searching under "teen suicide support." She had never used the word "support" in any of her searches before, but her gut told her to do so.

Surprised, she discovered there were chat forums for parents dealing with the suicide of their children. The thought that there were others like her felt both comforting and scary at the same time. Would they confirm what she felt about herself?

She almost clicked on a link to take her to one of the support sites, but then she heard the distant murmurings of Sean's voice coming from the kitchen area. She looked at the clock, surprised that Sean was up already. He'd never been one for the early morning hours. Unless he'd changed. What did she really know about her other son?

She turned off the computer and left the small home office she had fashioned for herself out of what had once been a breakfast nook and followed the sounds of Sean's voice.

She saw him leaning against the refrigerator, wearing his flannel robe and holding the phone with one hand and a cup of coffee with the other.

She wondered when Sean had begun to drink coffee. Didn't he hate coffee?

"Thanks for everything," Sean said into his cell phone, not noticing his mother's presence. "I…uh…miss you."

She saw a smile, the first since he'd been home, appear on Sean's face.

"Sorry for calling so early. I know what time it is there," Sean said. "I'll talk to you later."

He glanced up and saw his mother standing in the doorway.

"Morning," she said, red eyed from lack of sleep.

"Mom!" Sean said, looking shy suddenly. "Want some coffee?"

He motioned over to the almost near full pot he had brewed.

"Sure," she answered.

She watched as Sean poured her a cup and added two packs of sugar and a drop of milk in her coffee. How did he knew how she liked her coffee when she had no idea how he took his?

"Here ya go," Sean said, handing her the steaming mug.

"Thanks," she said. She took a sip of the piping hot liquid and felt the comfort that can come from some of the simplest things in life. "Talking to someone back in San Francisco?"

"Yep," he answered. He seemed to be hesitating as his eyes darted around the kitchen. "A guy I'm dating."

"Oh," she said.

She had never asked Sean about his love life. She didn't know how to go about doing it. Was it different in the "gay world?" She knew part of her felt scared to know the possible answer. Having your son tell you he's gay was very different than knowing for sure that your son had been having sex with another man.

Sean didn't know what to say next, so he filled his cup with more coffee.

Kate remembered how she always asked Matt about Alison, how she always had a present for Alison at Christmas, and made sure that Alison had been invited to family events.

"Have you been dating...him...for long?" Kate finally managed to ask.

Sean looked thrown by the question.

"Not long," he finally said. "But he's a great guy. I like him a lot."

Kate nodded.

"Good. I'm glad," she replied.

She then took another sip of the coffee her son had made.

"Hey, man," Brent said, sitting next to Javier at a picnic table outside of the school. "How you doin'?"

The bell had rung recently for break, and Javier had come outside looking for Alison. Often she sat under an oak tree in the front of the school during break and ate her usual Twix bar. But today she was nowhere to be seen.

"Hanging in there," Javier answered. "Sure you want to be seen with me? Feels like Alison and I are the new school pariahs. That is the right word, right? Pariahs?"

"People are just…I don't know…they don't know how to react to Matt killing himself," Brent said. He took a sour apple Jolly Rancher out of his pocket and popped it into his mouth. "Oh, and no, I'm not going anywhere. We're friends."

Javier relaxed for a second.

"Thanks, man," Javier said. "I appreciate it."

"Just do me a favor," Brent said.

"What's that?"

"Watch out for Beau," Brent replied. "From what I hear he wants to avenge Matt's death somehow."

"I can't spend all my time worried about Beau. I'm worried the most about Alison," Javier replied.

"Alison?" her friend Missy said, knocking softly on the bathroom stall door. "Are you okay?"

Alison had locked herself in the stall in the middle of second period feeling like she would vomit at any second. She couldn't remember the last time she had eaten a real meal. Ever since Matt's suicide, everything, even water sometimes, made her nauseous.

She stood next to the toilet, her back up against the wall, not wanting to come out and face anyone.

"Alison?" Missy asked again. "It's okay. I'm the only one in here. I checked in the other stalls to be sure."

Everyone knew that the girls' bathroom was gossip central. Words that had been overheard in the bathroom had ruined more than one high school student's reputation.

Alison tentatively unlocked the stall door and opened it. Missy stood there, genuine worry apparent on her face, wringing her hands.

"What are you doing?" she asked. "You disappeared right in the middle of second period."

"I don't know what to do," Alison said quietly.

"Ah, sweetie," Missy said, grabbing her hand and gently pulling her from the stall. "You can't hide in her all day, though."

"I can't be in this place. I can't take the stares and the whispers," Alison said. She walked over to the sink and splashed some cold water on her face.

"Your make-up!" Missy exclaimed.

"I've got much bigger shit to worry about than my make-up," Alison replied, pulling out a paper towel from the dispenser and drying her face.

"I'm sorry," Missy said, her head hanging.

"No, I'm sorry," Alison said, turning back around towards her friend. "I don't mean to snap. It's just so hard to be here. Missy, I don't know if I can make it."

They heard footsteps outside the bathroom door, but luckily no one came inside.

"You're strong, Alison," Missy said.

"Strong?" Alison said, almost laughing.

"You are," Missy said seriously. "You've always been so independent. Ever since we were little girls. The cool thing about you has always been that, sure, you were popular, but you didn't seem to work at it or really care. You've always done exactly what you wanted to do."

"Yeah, I broke up with Matt, and you see where that got me."

"It's not your fault what Matt did," Missy said, pausing before asking, "Have you thought about talking to one of the counselors the school offered everyone?"

"Do you think a counselor would do any good?" Alison asked.

Hesitating for a second, Missy said, "A counselor helped me a lot with my eating disorder."

Alison took a small step back. She never knew Missy had an eating disorder.

"Just promise me you'll think about it," Missy pleaded. "Just talking about things to someone who, I don't know, I guess isn't involved personally can really help."

Alison nodded her head and took a deep breath.

"I'll think about it," she replied.

The bell for the next period rang.

"Ugh, chemistry next," Missy groaned.

Alison took her friend's hand and squeezed it.

"Thanks for sticking by me," Alison said.

Missy smiled. "Of course, friends forever and ever, now..."

"And always," Alison finished, from their secret slogan they had created for their friendship back in second grade.

Robert had emerged from the bedroom by noon. Kate took this as a good sign. Better to sleep it off than drive off drunk to scream at employees. So she took it upon herself to cook lunch for her, Robert, and Sean. Cooking had never been her forte, but she needed to keep her hands busy.

"Lunch is ready!" she called out, trying a little too hard to sound at least a drop enthusiastic.

Robert shuffled to the kitchen table, wearing boxers and a gray t-shirt, as if on autopilot. Sean entered the kitchen dressed in a crisp blue oxford and jeans.

"You cooked, Mom?" Sean asked, sounding surprised.

"It's been known to happen," Kate replied. "Have a seat."

She then served everyone grilled cheese with tomato, a side salad of spinach and fresh avocado, and iced tea. She almost automatically pulled out a fourth plate for Matt. Then she remembered.

Sean started to eat his sandwich, chewing slowly, as if to test its edibility. He then smiled.

"It's good," he said.

"Thank you," Kate said, taking a seat at the table. She turned to Robert who sat in silence, not touching his food. "How are you feeling today?"

"Just great," he said sarcastically.

An uncomfortable, smothering silence enveloped the room.

"I thought maybe we could get out of the house today. Take a walk on the beach or something. The three of us," Kate said hopefully.

Robert picked at his salad.

"Don't feel like it. Maybe I'll go check on the site," Robert said.

Kate shifted uncomfortably in her chair.

Sean took a sip of tea. His mother had told him what had happened at the worksite earlier.

"I'm not sure if that's such a good idea," Kate said.

"And why is that?" Robert asked, challenging her.

"Enrique has things under control. I called him this morning. Best to let them keep on task."

"I own the goddamn construction company," Robert scowled.

"We own it," Kate corrected, surprising herself.

"Maybe Mom's right," Sean said, attempting to intervene. "It would probably do us all some good to get out of the house."

Kate watched Robert stare angrily across the table at Sean.

"When are you going back to California?" Robert said.

"Robert!" Kate exclaimed.

"I'm just saying," Robert began. "You hardly ever stuck around before. Why do so now?"

Sean could feel the internal rage he tried so hard to always keep buried make his way up his spine.

"Maybe there's a reason for that," Sean said coldly.

"To be with your kind?" Robert said. "That's the reason you went there. Right? So why don't you just go back?"

"Robert, stop this! Now!" Kate commanded.

"Believe it or not, dad, gay people are everywhere. Even here in Long Beach," Sean said.

"Whatever," Robert said. He waved his hand as if to disregard Sean.

"You know," Sean began, "you're right. I don't know why I try. The only son you cared about anyway is dead now."

Kate could feel the tears stinging her eyes. She willed them not to flow. She had cried too much the past few days. If she started again, she may not be able to stop.

"You said it," Robert said.

"I'm getting out of here. I don't have to take this. I'm not a child anymore," Sean said. He stood up and marched out of the room.

Kate heard his footsteps pounding up the stairs.

Just like Matt's that night, she thought, when he headed up to the study.

That night, she hadn't followed him even though she knew how upset he looked.

If only she had followed him.

Kate stood up, shoved her chair back under the table, and headed towards the foyer.

"Where are you going?" Robert demanded.

Kate paused for a second.

"A place I should have gone many years ago," she replied, thinking of a similar fight Sean and Robert had had over a dinner back when Sean had been Matt's age.

At lunchtime, Javier sat at a small side table with Brent and Adriana, the three of them eating slices of pizza with questionable cheese. Javier began to notice how Adriana, who rarely socialized with him at school, magically appeared quite frequently now whenever he hung out with Brent. Could his sister possibly have a crush on his friend? He didn't know how he felt about that.

"I wish people would stop staring over here," Adriana said. "Ever since that kid offed himself, I feel like people are constantly whispering around me."

"Just ignore them," Brent suggested. "I know it's easier said than done, but they're the ones with the problem."

If only it were that easy, Javier thought.

Finally he saw Alison. She headed over to the table with a determined look on her face.

"Hey," she said to him.

"Hey," Javier replied.

"Could we go outside to talk?" she asked.

"What do you want to talk to my brother about?" Adriana snapped.

"Adriana!" Javier exclaimed, but part of him felt supported. He knew she was acting loyal and protective in her own way.

"She's bought our family enough trouble already," Adriana said.

"I'm sorry," Alison began, "I didn't mean to…"

"It's okay," Javier said.

He glanced at Brent and Adriana and then back at Alison.

"Sure," he answered. "Let's go."

They headed to the football stadium out back and sat on one of the front row bleachers. Empty popcorn containers and soda cups from the last football game still littered the concrete floor.

"I've been thinking," Alison started.

"About?" Javier asked.

He noticed her lack of eye contact.

"Just with Matt's death and everything, maybe we should take things slower."

"Slower?"

"Yeah, I have so much going through my head right now," Alison said. She looked up at him and into those dark brown eyes that had drawn her to him in the first place. She didn't want to do this, but fear overcame her now just thinking about becoming involved with someone else. Maybe her father was right. "I'm not sure if this is the best time for me to get involved with someone else."

Javier swallowed hard and looked away. He didn't want her to see his disappointment.

"Sure," he said. "I understand. If that's what you want to do."

"It is," Alison said, but inside she knew she was nowhere near certain.

"Well," Javier said, suddenly looking at his watch. "Lunch will be over soon. Guess I better head back in. I need to get a book out of my locker."

He stood up and started to walk away.

"Javier!" Alison called out quickly.

He turned around.

"Yeah?" he said. He knew his voice sounded a little too hopeful, and this embarrassed him.

"I do like you," Alison said. "A lot. It's just things are so difficult now."

He nodded and walked off.

Alison sat for a few more moments. If this had been the right decision, why did it feel so wrong? But she figured there was no going back now.

Kate walked into the guest room to find Sean packing his bags with a look of fierce determination.

"Please, don't leave," Kate pleaded.

Sean picked a duffel bag up off the floor and began to fill it with underwear and socks.

"It's time, Mom," he said.

Kate sat on the edge of the bed and watched him continue to pack.

"Your father doesn't know what he's saying. He's been drinking so much," she said, trying to sound convincing.

"He knows exactly what he's saying. The difference is now I don't have to listen to it," Sean replied.

"Please, just stay a little longer."

"I just can't. I don't feel comfortable here."

He stopped packing and sat down next to her.

"Look, you can call me anytime. You could even come to San Francisco for a while if you wanted. But I just can't stay here and be constantly reminded by my father what a failure I am."

"Your father doesn't think you're a failure," Kate countered. But she wasn't sure if she believed the words herself as she spoke them.

"Matt was Dad's world. We both know that. I'm just serving as a reminder of what he doesn't have anymore, and my life just isn't here now."

He placed his hand on top of hers and squeezed it gently.

"I'm sorry," he said quietly before zipping up his suitcase.

Chapter 12

The weeks passed slowly by, and before Kate knew it Thanksgiving was just a day away. As the days had gone by she watched Robert continue to drink himself into oblivion. She finally had to take over most of his duties at the office, adding even more to her stress. Thank God for Enrique, she thought. He'd taken on quite a bit more, too, and he worked great with the crews.

What amazed Kate the most, though, was that as time went by it seemed life just went on, regardless of the fact that her son had killed himself: she still ran into people she knew who didn't know exactly what to say to her at the supermarket.

People usually approached her exactly as Marie Henson from her church social group did at the cleaners the other day. Marie walked up, a look of sadness and pity on her face, and said, "How are you doing, dear, with everything?"

Neither Marie nor anyone else mentioned Matt by name or God forbid use the "s" word, suicide. Instead, they talked around the issue.

"If you need anything at all, just let me know," Marie had said. "I make a wonderful tuna casserole."

As if a tuna casserole could right all the wrongs in Kate's world! Was the woman crazy?

Kate realized people just didn't know what to say, but she found herself wishing people would talk about it. How refreshing it would be to have someone walk up to her and say, "You know, I'm so sorry Matt shot himself in the head. Life must be beyond tough right now for you."

Now with the holidays approaching, Kate found herself even more at a loss. People around her were thankful for the fact that they had actually just survived a year in a post-Katrina Mississippi world. Life went on. People had business to take care of, such as the rebuilding of their homes, securing new work, still cleaning storm-wrecked areas. Matt's death had become almost a footnote in what had been a tragedy-filled past year and a half.

One morning while she sat on her front porch – that Robert had designed to look exactly like the one on their pre-storm house – she held the cordless phone in her hand and let her fingers roam over the numbers as she considered calling the suicide support group she had located in New Orleans. Her fear of the unknown, of having to face certain facts, paralyzed her when it came to dialing that number, and she placed the phone on the table next to her chair.

Enrique walked into the kitchen doorway and watched as Carmen, unaware of his presence, stuffed the turkey for tomorrow. As if the turkey were still alive, she delicately filled the cavity with her special cranberry stuffing. Even now, after all of these years, and with Carmen standing in the kitchen wearing an apron and a gloved hand covered with stuffing, Enrique wondered if there could ever possibly be a more beautiful woman than his wife.

With Robert's absence from work, Enrique found himself working twelve to fourteen hour days just to keep up. Carmen never once complained, and she made sure everything on the home front ran just as smooth as ever.

He knew she missed him, though, as he did her. They communicated this every morning without words when he kissed her goodbye after she had insisted on getting up with him to make his coffee and pack his lunch.

"Hang in there," she'd often tell him.

"When this is done we're going to take a nice vacation together, just the two of us," he promised.

Carmen turned around to pick up another bowl and jumped when she saw her husband in the doorway.

"Enrique!" she exclaimed. "You scared me! Why didn't you say anything?"

"I was watching you work," he said.

Carmen scratched her cheek and in the process left a small chunk of stuffing on the tip of her nose.

Enrique chuckled and walked up to her. He wiped the stuffing off her nose and gave her a gentle kiss.

"Well, this is a nice surprise," she said, looking at the clock. "You're home so early."

"Tomorrow's Thanksgiving, and the crew deserves a break after working six days a week lately. So, I let everyone go and came home, too."

"Good," Carmen said, smiling. "You can help me with the pies."

"No rest for the weary, huh?" he said. "Okay."

In fact, Enrique actually liked helping her make the pies every year at Thanksgiving. They both knew this even though it had never been verbalized.

"There's something I want to talk to you about first, though," he said. He pulled a chair out from under the kitchen table and motioned for her to take a seat too.

"Is something wrong?" Carmen asked.

"No, no, mi corazón," he began. "I got a call today from Ed Martinez back in L.A. He has the lead on a possible job for me in El Paso."

"El Paso?"

"It's a project to start in the new year. It's not definite, but it looks like it's headed that way. The money would be good. I probably wouldn't have to work as much, and…"

"And what?" Carmen asked.

"It's El Paso. We'll live in a city with a large number of Latinos again,' Enrique said, then paused before adding, "Sometimes I do worry about the children and if this was the right move - for all of us."

"Well, I know it's been hard on them, especially Adriana and Javi. But maybe in the end it'll make them stronger. I know I do miss being surrounded with Latin culture, though. This place is so different for all of us. So...small town. And so much fried food! Is there anything these people won't batter up and deep fry?"

"I miss *carne asada*," Enrique said. "I miss so many of the little things. What do you think we should do?"

She placed a hand on his knee and grinned.

"See what happens. If the project's a go, we can make a decision then. In the meantime, we can think about it. Talk to the kids if it looks serious."

He nodded.

"I only want what's best for the family," he said.

"I know, Enrique. I know."

Enrique suddenly noticed the complete lack of noise in the house.

"Where are the kids?" he asked.

"Javi went to the park with his friend, Brent. Adriana and a new friend went to the mall, and Ever is watching a movie over at a friend's house."

"So, we're actually alone?" Enrique said, cocking an eyebrow.

"Yes," she said. She recognized the particular gleam in his eye. "Alone at least for another hour or so."

"Are you thinking what I'm thinking?" he asked.

"I'm thinking the turkey and the pies can wait," Carmen said, grabbing her husband's hand.

"Goal!" Javier yelled in his one-on-one soccer game with Brent in the park. He picked up the soccer ball and bounced it in the air.

Brent, exhausted, collapsed on the cool grassy ground of the city park, recently reopened after the storm.

"Man, you're killing me. I can't even get one stupid-ass goal in!" Brent said.

Javier grabbed the ball and sat next to Brent on the grass.

"Don't feel bad, man," he said. "I'm Latin. This whole soccer thing is in my blood."

"Yeah, whatever," Brent teased. "I think you've got the ball under some weird kinda supernatural power."

"Dude, I think you're confusing my culture with some of that voodoo stuff in New Orleans."

Javier looked up and across the park he saw Alison walking her family's poodle.

"Ah, shit," Javier said under his breath.

"What?" Brent asked, sitting up.

"Alison's over there walking her dog," Javier said, looking over in Alison's direction.

Since their talk on the stadium bleachers the two hadn't really spoken except for awkward hellos in the hallway.

"Maybe you should go say hi," Brent suggested.

Javier looked as if he may be considering it for a second, but then he shrugged his shoulders.

"Nah, she's busy," he said.

"What? Walking her dog?" Brent said. "Come on, man. You know you want to."

Just then from across the way, the children's swing set between them, Alison glanced over and saw Javier staring at her. She hesitated and then waved at him.

Javier waved back.

"Go, man," Brent urged.

Alison stood still for a moment, but then she started walking off again with the dog.

"There she goes," Javier said, disappointed.

"Got everything packed?" Caleb asked Sean. "We can catch the next BART out to Pleasantville."

"I think so," Sean said, picking up his overnight bag off of his bed.

Caleb took his hand and started to lead him to the bedroom door, but Sean stayed glue to his spot.

"Can I be honest?" Sean asked.

"Of course," Caleb said.

"I'm pretty nervous about this," Sean admitted.

"Sean, my parents are going to love you," Caleb said, reassuringly. "You know why?"

"Why?"

"Because I'm nuts about you. That's why."

"Still, I hate to feel like I'm imposing."

Caleb sighed.

"First off, you're my boyfriend, and I want to spend Thanksgiving with you. Second, you are not spending Thanksgiving alone. You've been through a lot these past couple of months."

Sean didn't know what he would have done without Caleb's support since Matt's death. Caleb had been Sean's rock, and finally Sean had given in to his feelings for Caleb, not wanting to fight them anymore but to embrace them. If his brother's death taught him anything, it was to cherish each day.

"You're so sweet to me," Sean said, kissing him.

He only wished he had a family like Caleb's, one that he could bring a boyfriend home to meet.

Sitting in the back of her parent's car, watching the endless pine tress along the side of Highway 49 while headed to her grandmother's in Jackson for Thanksgiving, Alison's thoughts stayed on Javier. She could kick her own ass for not saying something to him at the park. But then how could she? She'd been the one to break it off with him, but she had regretted it ever since. She couldn't believe she listened to her father regarding her love life. After all, if she didn't date Javier, it wouldn't bring Matt back. So why should she deny her feelings?

She pulled out her iPOD to drown out the twangy country music her father insisted on playing all the way to Jackson, and she made a vow to herself. She'd find the courage to tell Javier how she really felt, and she'd hope that it wasn't too late.

Chapter 13

"What are you doing?" Robert demanded.

Kate turned around from assembling the Christmas tree in the living room. She had dragged the tree, all the decorations and the lights down from the attic by herself. That had always been Matt's job. He always loved helping Kate put up the tree.

"What does it look like I'm doing? I'm putting up the Christmas tree. There's only a couple of weeks left," Kate answered. She turned back to continue adding branches to the artificial tree.

She had felt the ocean of disconnect between her and Robert growing wider and deeper with each day. Robert often spent days at the golf course or more likely drinking at the bar in the country club where the course was located. Kate became consumed with keeping the business afloat, meeting deadlines and dealing with vendors. Robert, oddly enough, appeared to care less. He never even asked her how the project was going.

Kate knew she had stopped reaching out to her husband, too. She told herself she was simply too busy trying to keep their business going, but deep down she still felt racked with guilt. She'd known something had been terribly wrong. She'd known and did nothing.

"Not in this house," Robert said. "Not this year."

"Matt would want a tree up," Kate said casually.

She opened a box and took out a tangled ball of tree lights.

"Matt's not here," Robert said, matter of fact.

Kate froze for a moment and looked across the room, suddenly in a stand-off with Robert.

"Well, if Matt was here, he'd want a tree up. So, I'm putting the goddamn tree in the living room!"

"Not while I'm here," Robert challenged.

"Well, I guess that's up to you," Kate replied, then watched as Robert stormed out.

"Did you decide if you're going home at all yet?" Caleb asked, surveying the completed Christmas trimming work.

The two had just returned from a Christmas tree lot in the Noe Valley. Caleb had insisted he wanted a real tree this year so he could smell the fresh pine scent throughout his apartment. Sean had told him that cutting down trees didn't exactly help the environment. Caleb had countered that producing more plastic for imitation trees didn't exactly help matters either. Eventually, Caleb had agreed to recycle the tree by giving it to the neighborhood garden for fertilizer after the season ended.

While Christmas carols played and the two of them drank extra spiced eggnog, they decorated the tree together, and for the first time in a long time, Sean realized that he had gone a long while without thinking about things back home. But now Caleb had brought it back to the forefront again.

"I don't think so," Sean shrugged. "I think I'll do better sticking around here."

"What about your parents?" Caleb said, quietly.

Sean straightened the angel on top of the tree while he chose his words carefully.

"I think it'll be better without me there this year," he replied.

"Why?" Caleb said, walking up behind Sean and wrapping his arms around his waist.

Sean broke from the embrace.

"Caleb, my family isn't like yours, okay? It just isn't," he said.

Over Thanksgiving, Sean had been overwhelmed by how Caleb's family had greeted and welcomed him into their home. Caleb's father didn't even miss a beat when he led Caleb and Sean down the hall to "their room."

"I'm sorry, sweetie," Caleb said, reaching out for Sean's hand. "I know this will be a tough time of year for you. Whatever you decide, I'll support you, of course."

But later that night, after Caleb had fallen asleep with his head laying in Sean's lap as they watched "Miracle on 34th Street", Caleb's words echoed in Sean's head. He thought about his parents and wondered if he should make the effort after all. Maybe if he went for just a couple of days, nothing too long, and had a presence, it would help all three of them in some way.

He carefully reached over Caleb's head, grabbed his cell phone from the coffee table, and dialed his mother's cell number.

After enough rings went by that Sean figured he would get voicemail, his mother picked up at the last second.

"Hello? Sean?" she said.

"Hi, Mom," Sean said softly, to not wake Caleb. "How are you?"

"Oh, well, I'm here. I'm here," she repeated.

"Are you guys going to be home for Christmas?"

Silence on the other end of the phone.

"Mom? Are you there?"

"I'm here," Kate said finally.

"Is something wrong?"

"Your father is gone. So, I guess he won't be here for Christmas."

It took Sean a few seconds to process what his mother had just said.

"What do you mean by 'gone'?"

"He left a note on the kitchen counter for me, saying he needed some space and would be gone for a while."

He could hear his mother's voice beginning to crack.

"Maybe he just meant for a day or so," Sean said.

"I don't think so."

"Why?"

"He signed the note with Happy New Year," she answered.

In the living room, sitting on the couch, Javier worked on his geometry. Ever sat in front of the living room TV eating popcorn sprinkled with sugar and watching "Rudolph the Red Nosed Reindeer" on DVD. Adriana sat by him painting her nails a new shade of pink. The twinkling lights of the Christmas tree next to them illuminated the room in alternating green and red light.

"Kids," Enrique said, entering the room with Carmen by his side. "We need to talk to you about something."

"Oh, no," Adriana groaned. "What's wrong now?"

Javier put down his geometry book. "What's going on? Is everyone okay?

"Ever, sweetie, can you turn the TV off for a second?" Carmen asked.

Ever did as he was told while Enrique and Carmen sat next to each other on the love seat.

"You guys look so serious," Javier said.

"Everything's okay," Enrique began.

"There's just something we want to talk to you about," Carmen said.

Ever swallowed a mouth full of popcorn. "What is it?"

"I might be getting a good job offer in El Paso," Enrique said. "If that happens, your mother and I are talking about moving to Texas."

"Texas!" Javier exclaimed. "We just moved here."

"Yes, we know," Carmen said. "It's a good job offer though, and…"

"Your mother and I have been wondering if we might all feel more comfortable in Texas."

"You mean because there'll be a lot of other Latinos?" Adriana asked.

Enrique nodded. "Well, for one thing. There are others."

"Ultimately, the decision will be ours, but we want to know what you kids think," Carmen said.

Silence overtook the room as all three of the kids went deep into thought.

"Why can't we just go back to L.A.?" Adriana asked. "I just sort of got used to here. If we moved to El Paso, we'll have to start all over. Again!"

"Your father is going where there is good work, *mija*," Carmen said. "You know that."

Adriana groaned and looked down at her newly-painted nails as if it had all been a waste of time.

"I like it here!" Ever interjected. "I can ride my bike all over the neighborhood.

"Javier?" Enrique asked.

Javier shrugged his shoulders.

"Whatever you think is best, *Papi*," he said. But his first thought had been of Alison.

"Hey there!" Alison called out to Javier after school the next day.

She saw him leaving school and starting his walk home, and at that moment she decided she'd be brave. She had to tell him what she felt even if it meant he said no. At least then she would know.

Javier stopped on the sidewalk.

"Hey," he said.

"Okay if I walk with you?" she asked, running up to meet him.

"Really?" Javier asked, surprised. "It's a little out of your way, isn't it?"

"I don't mind," she said.

Javier stuffed his hands in his front pockets and looked around. Those familiar butterflies in his stomach that appeared whenever Alison was present began to stir again at a feverish pace.

"Sure then," he said.

For a few moments they said nothing as they walked, until Alison asked, "Is your family staying here for Christmas or going back to Los Angeles?"

"We'll be here," he answered. "Yours?"

"Yeah," Alison replied. "We always stick around."

When they reached the crosswalk, Alison stopped.

"Is it okay if I ask you something?" she said.

"Sure," Javier said.

"Do you ever think about me, I mean us?"

Javier took a deep breath.

"Sometimes," he said. All the time, he thought.

"After what Matt did, I was so messed up, Javier. It's not that I didn't want to date you, but I blamed myself partly for what Matt did, and the idea of loving someone, loving you, scared me."

"Loving me?" Javier said, feeling a rush of warmth throughout his body.

"Yeah," Alison muttered. "The point is, I'm sorry. I shouldn't have ended things so quickly. I shouldn't have cared what anyone else thought about us or our relationship."

Javier wanted to grab her in his arms, kiss her, and tell her how much he'd missed her, but his pride kept his emotions in check.

"And now?" he asked.

"I'd like another chance. That is if you'd like to. Would you?" Alison asked, hopeful.

Javier smiled.

"I'd like that a lot," he answered.

Before he had finished answering, though, Alison had already embraced him and held on to him tightly, not wanting to ever let go.

Javier enjoyed her touch, her embrace, so much that he just couldn't bear to tell her that before long, he may be leaving.

Chapter 14

Sean paced back and forth in front of a newsstand at San Francisco International Airport. Caleb stood in line to purchase a copy of the San Francisco Examiner.

"We can find some cool events to take her to in the paper," Caleb had said.

Sean still couldn't believe his mother had taken him up on his offer to come stay in San Francisco for Christmas. He thought she'd decline politely, and that would be that. He would have done his duty as a son by offering. It saddened him to think of her staying alone in that huge house back in Long Beach over Christmas while his father was God knows where. It had never crossed his mind that his mother would have left, though, without waiting around to see if his father returned.

At first, Sean had hesitated in asking Caleb if he wanted to go to the airport with him to pick up his mother. But then, after thinking about it, he figured if she was coming into his territory, San Francisco, she would have to get used to all aspects of his life, including Caleb.

If Sean had been Caleb he wasn't sure he would have agreed to go the airport. Talk about possible drama! But Caleb had only said, "Sure. What time?"

"There she is!" Sean said, as Caleb returned to his side.

Kate, rolling her luggage behind her, and wearing a green pant suit with heels, had just walked out of the terminal. Only his mother would have worn high heels on a plane!

"Mom!" Sean called out. He had a sudden sinking feeling in his stomach. He just didn't know how, or if, he could pull this off.

She saw him, walked over, and gave him a hug.

"Hi, son," she said.

When she let Sean go she stepped back and looked at Caleb.

"Hi," Caleb said.

"Mom, this is…" Sean started to say.

"Caleb," Kate said. "It's nice to meet you."

She glanced back at Sean who had a worried look on his face. She then looked back at Caleb.

"Well, you certainly are very handsome," Kate said to Caleb. Caleb blushed.

"Why thank you," he said. "Do you need help with your bag?"

"That'd be great" Kate said, handing the luggage over. "I can't wait to see the city!"

As they walked towards the BART station to catch the train, Kate grabbed Sean's arm and said, "It's great to see you."

Sean, finally more relaxed, said, "You too, Mom."

Lying across the bed in his Natchez hotel room, Robert flipped through the channels on the TV, never stopping for more than a few minutes on any one channel. He hadn't left the room itself in a few days now. He shunned housekeeping when they came by each day with a loud, "Don't need anything, thanks!" For food, he had take-out delivered, not that he felt very hungry.

Everything went on the American Express, and he could have cared less what the bill ended up totaling. He just wanted to be away from everything that reminded him of his life back home, his broken family, and the son he had so cherished who felt the need to take his own life.

He got up off the bed and walked to the bathroom sink to pour some water in a plastic hotel cup. When he caught his reflection in the mirror, he almost did a double-take.

He kicked the towels on the floor out of his way and walked closer to the mirror.

His hands went to his face, touching it, almost as if to make sure that this reflection, this stranger, actually was him. He had almost grown a full beard at this point. His eyes were bloodshot and deep purple tones colored the skin immediately below. His hair, which he had always kept short and neat, looked haphazard now, sticking up in all directions.

He wanted to punch this man he saw in the mirror. He wanted to hit the mirror so hard until the pain from the impact wiped out all of the thoughts that had haunted him since his son took his life.

What kind of father was he that his own son would kill himself? What kind of father didn't notice what was going on? What kind of son would do that to this father? He had tried so hard to give Matt everything, all the opportunities he'd never had growing up. He wondered if he pushed his son too hard. Did his expectations of him prove to be too much for his son, or anyone for that matter, to live up to?

He couldn't stand looking at his wife, either, which had been the biggest reason he had to leave. It's not that he blamed Kate. But every time he saw her he remembered the conversation she had with him about something being wrong with Matt, and he ignored it. He had brushed it off and not been willing to even listen. How could he look his wife in the eye now after he had let his family down so much?

He thought of Sean running out of the kitchen that day. Why had he said what he did to him? He had never known how to deal with Sean, ever since he was a little boy. Robert hadn't admitted it, but he'd known on a deeper level that Sean would be different from most of the other boys, and this scared him. He hadn't known how to deal with, or even talk to, a son who had turned out so fundamentally different than he expected. Sitting in the hotel room in his self imposed solitary confinement, he thought nonstop about his failings as a husband and a father, and wondered what he could have done differently.

Unfortunately, no answers came to him, only feelings of guilt, resentment, and anger.

He turned the bathroom light off so he couldn't see his reflection any more and headed back to the bed, forgetting about his water.

While riding the streetcar up steep Nob Hill in San Francisco, Kate closed her eyes and let the chilly Bay Area air hit her in the face. She hung on tightly to one of the poles and breathed the crisp air deeply. The rush of the streetcar's speed up the hill, along with sounds of the city mixed with the rush of air, had her feeling truly alive for the first time in months.

She turned her head and looked back at Sean and Caleb, who sat on a bench behind her, and smiled at them. They smiled back, and she wondered how she had allowed herself to go so long without coming to see the world her son lived in. Every time she'd mention to Robert that they should visit Sean in San Francisco, Robert would shoot the idea down, and she knew why. He didn't want to know about Sean's life in San Francisco.

She looked around at the city, the architecture, the energy in the air, and at Sean who had now taken Caleb's hand in his as if it were the most natural thing in the world. She knew then why he had come here and stayed, but with everything in her she wanted to bring her only remaining child back into her life. And to do this she needed to be honest with him – about everything.

The streetcar jerked to a stop, and Sean and Caleb got up.

"This is our stop," Sean said, as he took her arm and helped her step down from the streetcar.

"I hope you like Chinese food," Caleb said. "They have some of the best here in San Francisco."

"I'm sure I'll love it," she said, opening herself up to more possibilities.

***

"This is for you," Javier said, handing Alison a small wrapped box.

"You're so sweet!" she exclaimed.

"Merry Christmas," he said.

They sat on one of the few post-Katrina piers remaining in Biloxi on an unusually sunny day this close to Christmas.

The past few weeks had been some of the best Javier could remember. He felt high on the octane of falling in love. Sure, some people still gossiped behind their backs and tried to tie them to Matt's death, but the two of them had made a vow to focus on getting to know each other. Other people's opinions were simply that - theirs.

The thought that his family may be leaving for El Paso kept resurfacing in the back of Javier's mind. Before he had made the decision to tell Alison about the possibility, though, his parents had announced that they would be staying in Mississippi, at least until the end of the school year. They had decided that uprooting the kids in the middle of the school year may be too much, and once it was over they would then decide what to do. That meant Javier would be staying there for graduation with Alison. After then, of course, there would be college that could separate them, but then that could be true of any couple that fell in love during high school. He now had this time to get to know the girl who had captivated him from the first moment he saw her.

He watched as Alison opened the box with excited anticipation.

"I hope you like it," he said.

She opened it up and found a gold chain with a small heart-shaped pendant accented by a small diamond.

"Javier!" she exclaimed. "Wow…it's so…how did you?"

"Hey, you got a working man here," he joked. "I wanted to get you something special that you could keep close to your heart."

"It's beautiful!" she said. "Can you help me put it on?"

She lifted her hair, and he clasped the necklace.

"Thank you so much," she said. "It's been…a hard year in so many ways. But I'm glad I got you out of all of it."

"Would you have ever thought a year ago you'd be sitting here with a guy from L.A.?" he said, chuckling.

"Nope. It makes me wonder what other good surprises life might have in store for me," Alison said, and then she kissed him.

"Son, I can sleep on the couch," Kate said. "Really, it's fine."

"No, Mom. I'm not going to let you sleep on the couch," Sean replied, making his bed up for her. "I even changed the sheets for you."

"Oh, wow! Well, thanks!" she said, smiling. "Is your roommate ever here?"

"Not much," Sean said. "She's always traveling."

"Perfect roommate then," Kate said. She then sat on the bed and patted the space beside her. "Could we talk for a moment?"

"Sure," Sean said, sitting down. "Is everything okay?"

"I just want to tell you I think Caleb's great," she said. "I know we've never really talked much about your personal life."

"It's okay."

"No, it's not," she said, shaking her head. "Your brother's...death...has made me realize a lot of things in life, including that. I want to be part of your life, Sean. I need it, and, son, I can't say enough how sorry I am that I haven't been there all along."

Sean began to get choked up.

"I know my being gay hasn't been easy for y'all to deal with," he said. "But it's me."

"I know, baby. I just hope you'll give me a second chance to be the mother I haven't been lately," she said.

She then embraced him so hard Sean had to struggle for his breath.

"Of course, Mom," he said, hugging her back. "I'd like that. A lot in fact."

At that point, Kate began to sob into her son's shoulder.

"It's okay," Sean said. "We'll have plenty of time to get to know each other again."

"It's not just that, Sean," she said, pulling back. "There's something you don't know, something I haven't told anyone."

She looked away, and Sean reached out and turned her face back towards him.

"What is it?" he asked. "You can tell me."

She stood up and began pacing back and forth across the room, just like Sean did when he felt upset.

"I'm the reason he did it," she said.

"What are you talking about, Mom?"

She stopped pacing and faced her son. She had to say it, she had to get this off her chest, and she had to beg for his forgiveness.

"I'm the reason for Matt not being here," she said, before doubling over, falling to the floor and sobbing.

Sean rushed over and knelt down beside her.

"Mom, what are you talking about? You're not responsible for Matt killing himself," he insisted.

She realized Sean had said it. He'd verbalized it. Matt killed himself.

"Yes, I am!" she exclaimed. She stood up and started pacing again, her breath quickening, all of the emotions she had held on to for so long now bubbled at the surface, waiting to be released. "I knew something was wrong with Matt. I knew he wasn't happy. I found the razorblade!"

"Razorblade! What? Stop for a second," Sean said, grabbing onto her. "You're not making sense."

"I found a razorblade in his dresser drawer and everything in me told me something was wrong, and I tried to talk to your father about it. But…"

"But what?"

"I didn't try hard enough," she said, shaking her head. "I brushed it off. I told myself there was nothing to worry about even though I found that razorblade."

"Matt shot himself. What are you talking about a razor for?" Sean asked perplexed.

Kate wiped the tears from her eyes and sat down on the bed.

"Take a deep breath, and tell me what's going on," Sean said.

She tried to steady herself, her breathing, her thoughts. She had told no one, not even Robert.

"After Matt died, killed himself," she began, "the investigator told me they found cut marks on his body. Matt was a cutter."

"A cutter?" Sean said, shaking his head. The term sounded somewhat familiar, but he didn't know from where. "What is that?"

"Someone who cuts themselves intentionally to take their mind off of what they're feeling. I've been reading a lot on the internet. Some people do it to feel in control."

"Matt was cutting himself," Sean repeated.

"You know we never talked with him about how he felt after the storm. Hell, we never talked about how it made any of us feel, and he was the one that had to be pulled from the house. Oh, God! He must have been so scared, Sean. He didn't know where we were. He didn't know if he'd live. He was never the same after that. Never! I should have done something. And when I found that razorblade I still did nothing. I just…please forgive me."

"Look," Sean began. "You are not responsible for what Matt did."

"How can you say that?"

"Because it's the truth!" Sean exclaimed. "Mom, the person who killed Matt was Matt. He may not have been in his right frame of mind when he did, but it was his decision. Don't think I haven't tried to blame myself for what he did, too."

"You have?" Kate said shocked. "But why?"

"I've wondered what I could've said, could've done. Maybe if I had tried to get to know him more, be a better brother."

"Sweetie, it's not your fault!"

"I know that now," Sean said. "Between Caleb being there for me, and, well…I've been seeing a counselor, too."

"Really?" Kate said sitting straight up. How many times had she agonized over whether to make that call for information on the support group?

"Yeah. Caleb talked me into it, and it was the best thing I could have done. I think it would help you, too, to see that what happened is not your fault."

"I don't know if I can ever think that," she admitted.

"It may not happen overnight, and it may not happen for a while, but we need to get you help. I'll help you find a therapist to go to back home. But, Mom," Sean said urgently, "Matt's suicide is not your fault."

Still unconvinced, she looked away.

"I haven't told your father about Matt's cutting. I just couldn't do it. I was so afraid he'd blame me, just like I blamed myself and it would make things even worse. But now your father left, and I just didn't know how to talk to him anymore."

"He's having a hard time dealing with it, too. I mean I didn't tell the two of you about my being in counseling because we never talked about things like that. Dad always acted like people who did that were weak, but we've got to work on healing, forgiving ourselves, and ultimately forgiving Matt."

Sean held her close to him again.

"And we'll do it together, me and you, and hopefully, maybe, one day Dad."

Chapter 15

"Woohoo!" Javier yelled from along Beach Boulevard as he watched the fireworks across Bay St. Louis with Alison, Brent, and his sister.

"2007. Finally." Alison said, turning and planting a deep kiss on Javier.

"A brand new year!" Javier exclaimed, looking around for Brent and Adriana. "Hey, where's my sister and…"

Alison nudged him in the side and pointed over to a grassy area of the beach.

"Look," she said, pointing.

Javier turned to see Brent and Adriana holding hands and watching the fireworks.

"Oh, man. Thank God Dad's not here to see this!" Javier commented.

"I think they look cute together."

Javier sighed. "Yeah, I guess Brent's a good enough guy for my little sister. He just better treat her right. She may drive me freaking nuts, but she's still my little sister."

"And that's one of the things I like so much about you," Alison said, grinning.

***

"I can't believe you're actually letting Javier and Adriana stay out until one," Carmen said.

"Yeah, well, guess they caught me in a good mood," Enrique said, as they watched the fireworks from their backyard in their swing. "Besides, I didn't see you objecting, either."

"Well, with Ever at a sleepover I thought it would be nice just to have some us time," she said.

Enrique reached down to the ground and picked up a bottle of champagne and poured two glasses.

"And this is for you, pretty lady," he said, handing Carmen one of the glasses.

"Thank you," she said.

Enrique took a huge swallow, but Carmen just sat next to him not even taking a sip.

"You don't want any?" he asked.

"Can't," she replied.

"Why not?" he asked.

"It's not good for the baby," she said.

Enrique stopped in mid-sip.

"Are you saying what I think you're saying?" he asked, sitting straight up in the swing.

"Yep," Carmen answered. "It's another reason I wanted us to have some alone time tonight."

"We're going to have another baby?" he asked, still not completely believing it.

"I just took the test earlier this morning. A little bit of a surprise for 2007, huh?"

"I'll say," Enrique said, shaking his head.

"Are you happy about it?" Carmen asked, a little anxious.

Enrique jumped up from the swing, reached down, and lifted Carmen up in the air.

"Enrique!" Carmen yelled.

He then lowered her to him and began to kiss her passionately before saying, "I couldn't be a happier man. Just wouldn't be possible."

"I'm so glad," Carmen said, relieved. "God knows we weren't planning on it."

"Sometimes the best things that happen are unplanned," Enrique said, before kissing her again.

Sean and Caleb, cuddled up together in a blanket and sharing a bottle of Merlot, watched New Year's fireworks over the San Francisco Bay from the top of Caleb's apartment building.

"It's 2007," Caleb whispered into Sean's ear, holding him from behind.

"Thank God," Sean said. "2006 was a royal bitch, except for meeting you, of course. That I'm so thankful for."

"Me, too," Caleb said, before placing a kiss on Sean's cheek.

"I wish I could have talked Mom into staying for New Year's today. She kept saying she needed to go home and start dealing."

An extra spectacular display of red, gold, and green exploded in the sky with a loud pop.

"At least she knows she has you to lean on for support," Caleb said.

"When she shocked the hell out of me by saying she'd come to visit me I was so scared."

"I know," Caleb said, nodding.

"I'm so glad she did though. If she hadn't...well, it turned out to be so important for both of us. For the first time in I don't remember when we actually really talked, not talked around things."

This time a display of bright blue stars shot up in the sky, illuminating the top of the roof and bathing Sean and Caleb in its brilliance.

Exhausted after one flight delay after another, Kate arrived home in the middle of the night. She barely had enough mind power left to count out money for the cab driver who had picked her up from the Gulfport/Biloxi airport and now unloaded her luggage in front of her house.

"Here ya go," she said, handing him a twenty for a ten dollar fare. "Keep the change."

"Wow, thanks! Happy New Year to you!" the driver, a young guy who couldn't have been more than twenty-five, said to her.

"Happy New Year," Kate said softly.

She watched the driver take off, and she mustered up what energy she had left to haul her luggage into the house.

"Need some help, Katie?" she heard a familiar voice ask.

She turned to find Robert, clean shaven and actually looking sober, standing in the driveway.

"Robert!" she said. "You're here!"

"Yeah," he said. "Want to hear something funny?"

"I'd love to," she said in a half-whisper, still in awe that he stood before her.

"I had actually been sitting outside for the past two hours trying to get up the nerve to go inside to talk to you. I assumed you were home because of the light being on upstairs and your car here, and then all of a sudden you pull up in a cab," he said, walking closer to her. "And here you are, Katie."

She took a deep breath. He hadn't called her Katie since their courting days.

"I went to go visit Sean in San Francisco for Christmas."

"Really?" Robert asked, looking surprised. "How is he?"

"He's good, Robert. He's going to be okay."

Robert nodded.

"Good. I'm glad to hear that," he replied. "Are we going to be okay?"

"I hope so," she said, taken aback by his question. "It might take some time, though."

"I know. I realize that now. It's been hard, but I do."

Kate wrapped her arms around herself and began to shiver.

"Well, it's cold. Are you going to help me with this luggage or not?" she asked.

"Yes, ma'am," Robert said, hopping to duty and grabbing her bags.

They walked to the front door, together, and Kate took out her keys and unlocked it. She went inside and turned on the light, but she noticed Robert looked a little hesitant, maybe even a little scared.

"Well, you going to come in or what?" she asked.

"Yeah, I'm coming in," he said finally.

Robert then walked into the house to Kate and into the light.

Epilogue

Kate could still remember being a little girl and how disappointed she felt one steamy summer afternoon when her mother had taken her to the beach to build a sandcastle. Taking partial shelter under one of the big oak trees along the beach, the two of them watched what Kate had considered to be their best and most elaborate sandcastle ever. It had taken them a whole two hours to build, but quickly melted away during one of those Southern summer rain showers that can suddenly, and violently, pop up out of nowhere.

"I hate rain!" Kate had proclaimed. "We worked so hard!"

"We can come back another day before you go back to school," her mother said consolingly. "I promise."

"But it won't be the same, not like this one. We didn't even have time to play in it," Kate said, stomping her foot. "Stupid rain!"

"Ah, baby, it's okay," her mother had said. "Besides we have to embrace the rain. It might appear when we don't want it and change our plans but without it we wouldn't get the pretty flowers and the bright green grass in the yard you like to play in, either."

"I guess," Kate reluctantly agreed.

"You ready to make a run for it back home?" her mother had asked. "I'll make you a peanut butter and jelly sandwich."

Kate had nodded, brightening up a little.

"Hold on to my hand tight. We're going to run together. Okay?" her mother said, squeezing her hand tightly.

"Okay," Kate said, sort of looking forward to running home the four blocks in the rain. At least it would provide some relief from the unrelenting heat.

"I'm going to count to three," her mother began. "Then we'll make a big run for it. One."

Kate turned towards the sidewalk that would lead back to her house.

"Two," her mother said.

Kate readied herself for the downpour.

"Three!" her mother yelled loudly.

And off the two of them sprinted together, hand in hand.

About the Author

Michael Holloway Perronne's debut novel, A Time Before Me, was a finalist in Foreword Magazine's Book of the Year Award in 2006. His other works include Starstuck: A Hollywood Saga and Falling Into Me.

Originally from the South Mississippi and New Orleans area, Michael now calls Los Angeles home and is hard at work on his next novel, A Big Easy Christmas. For more information on Michael, please visit the author's website at www.michaelhperronne.com.

2783806

Made in the USA